MW01490986

AWAKENING STORM

THE DIVINE TREE GUARDIAN SERIES

LARISSA EMERALD

Awakening Storm
The Divine Tree Guardian Series, Book Three

by Larissa Emerald
Copyright © 2016 Castle Oak Publishing LLC

ISBN-10: 1-942139-13-6
ISBN-13: 978-1-942139-13-3

http://www.larissaemerald.com

Published in the United States of America.

Books by Larissa Emerald

Paranormal Romance

Divine Tree Guardian Series

Awakening Fire
Awakening Touch
Awakening Storm

Nocturne Falls Universe

The Vampire Bounty Hunter's Unexpected Catch
The Shaman Charms the Shifter

Vampire

Forever At Dawn – short
Forever At Midnight – short

Romantic Suspense

Winter Heat

Barefoot Bay – Kindle World

Come Sail Away – short

For my son Bryan
who has brought me love and laughter and challenges.

I love you beyond measure.

THE STORY

Time is running out for Rhianna Mori to give her beloved 96 year old grandfather what he wants most before he dies—the answer to what happened to his father. So when the Pilate instructor is chosen for the reality show If You Dare, she embarks on an adventure that's been a lifelong dream…to visit Japan, the land of her ancestors, and maybe, if she's lucky, be able to learn more about what happened to her lost great-grandfather.

From the moment she's dropped off on an uninhabited island located in the Dragon Vortex, a place where people disappear never to be heard from again, strange things occur. She quickly discovers the island isn't as deserted as she's told. And she soon encounters the tiger shifter, Divine Tree Guardian Aidan Hearst.

Aidan hopes the beautiful stranger on his island will pack up and leave before the sorceress of the alternate realm of Riam notices her presence and enslaves her. But the stubborn woman falls into the sorceress's trap despite his warnings. Dealing with his conflicting emotions, Aidan enters the evils of Riam to save Rhianna. Getting in is easy, getting out…will be another matter altogether. If not impossible. Especially before the Age of Atonement begins.

THE LEGEND

In the beginning of ancient time, the massive Tree of Life stood tall, with heavy branches and mile-deep roots, holding within knowledge of the universe. But after the division of good and evil, this sacred tree needed to be protected against exploitation and the Archangel Seth was charged with the tree's protection.

Realizing one such tree was far more susceptible to destruction than several, the angel split the tree into twelve that took root around the globe; if one tree should fall, the knowledge of the universe would prevail within its colleagues.

The archangel created a brotherhood of powerful immortal guardians to safeguard the mighty trees. These twelve brothers, from the Isle of Skye, formed the league of the Divine Tree Guardians.

Awakening Storm

Prologue

Theodora extended her scepter, pointing it at the man who was flexing his muscles and puffing out his chest as he stood defiantly before her. He obviously didn't understand that she was the person to please in Riam. Moloch the Demon Prince himself had tethered her to the alternate universe, and she would rule it as she wished. It didn't matter that it was a punishment; she was the most powerful being in the realm.

He'd been her lover once. Back then he had truly cared for her and had gifted her with the powers of sorcery, back before she'd made that teeny mistake of falling into bed with his demon brother.

She released a venomous grumble. Every time she thought about it, anger boiled to the surface of her skin. Moloch had maimed her, slicing her with his sword across her shoulder and breasts. She had healed, but the scars were thick, ugly, and permanent. He'd incarcerated her here in the alternate universe, Riam, then allowed her only

600,000 measly square miles of ocean from which to apprehend her subjects. After all, what was a queen without her subjects?

Unfortunately, this stretch of ocean wasn't very fruitful. She slammed the tip of her staff against the dusty ground. As if many humans passed through the Dragon Vortex!

Her lips twisted into a smirk. At least the name people had given the place was pleasing.

The large man moved before her, drawing her attention back to him. With a swirl of electric-blue energy from her scepter, she lifted him off his feet and held him there. The pained, panic-stricken expression on his face was priceless. When she grew tired of holding her arm up, she let him fall. He immediately crumpled to the ground.

"Stand," she ordered.

Slowly, he did. This time with none of the confidence he had before. She could smell the acrid scent of fear wafting from his skin. "I am your ruler now. When I say fight, you will fight. To the death."

He dipped his head, acquiescing to her command.

That's much better.

She dropped a broad sword at his feet and then lifted her chin, smiling, satisfied the war would go on. She floated to her spectator's booth and got comfortable. All eyes were on her as she raised the scepter in the air and then let if fall with a crack of thunder.

"Let the war games begin!" she shouted with glee.

The men and women started attacking one another ruthlessly. She liked to pick a favorite, someone vicious and capable of amassing a lot of kills. She scanned the havoc before her, searching for her victor. Screams, sobs, and the sound of bleeding hearts filled her ears.

She wished the game could go on and on. Unfortunately, she'd had to come up with viable game rules, as it were. Since her subjects were limited by supply, each game was shorter than she'd like. And when the game was over, she had to use her magic to revive those who had lost. At least their pain was palpable as they came to life once more.

As the dead began to rise with tortured wails, she smiled before addressing her people. "Now go. Live to battle another day."

1

The pup tramped in a happy circle. Even with the slap of the surf against the hull, Aidan's superior hearing distinguished the clacking sound of the dog's nails over the fiberglass deck. Pup snapped his head around and peered at Aidan with trusting chocolate eyes. After three failed attempts to jump onto Aidan's lap, the animal finally pawed his way up and was resting on his thighs. He hung his gigantic front feet over Aidan's arm as it draped over the steering wheel, guiding the sailboat's passage back to his home on the remote island of Tsuriairando.

"I can't keep calling you 'Pup.'" Aidan stared across the thrashing waves, thinking. "Takeshi. You will be Takeshi. *Warrior.*" He let the name roll over his tongue, pleased with the symbolism. It reminded him of the early days in Scotland, when he and his brothers protected the moors from invaders, a time long before they had become Divine Tree Guardians.

Aidan could use a warrior at his side to help fight the

current rise of evil that preceded the Age of Atonement. His brothers had revealed as much during their Guardian Congress last month. All eleven of them had agreed to the monthly meetings following Ian's recent encounter with a reaper in France. The increased communications would help them stay ahead of their enemies. Hopefully.

Aidan stroked Takeshi's brindled, salt-dampened fur, allowing his gaze to sweep the ocean as far as the eye could see. His island, the place where his Divine Tree resided, was about six hundred miles east of Yamada, a fishing town in Japan, and he was its only inhabitant. He had to sail a full twenty-six hours to reach his island home from his modest mainland home where his *delegato*, or assistant, Naoki resided. It was a trip Aidan only made about three times a year. Naoki generally kept him supplied with everything he could want or need. But Aidan had wanted to pick up the Akita pup himself. Naoki had found him as a possible replacement for the dog Aidan had lost in months before. And as always, his *delegato* had chosen well.

Aidan stroked Takeshi again. He had lost many animal friends over his centuries as Guardian, but he still remembered and treasured every one.

The pup barked at the flap and crack of the sails. A series of storms had been predicted, and it was already clear that a gray and windy day loomed before them. The waves peaked higher the farther he navigated into the Pacific. Takeshi licked Aidan's face and then wagged his tail with pent-up energy.

"When we get home, I'll introduce you to the tiger and eagle. Then we can run the entire island," Aidan told him.

Takeshi barked again, making Aidan laugh. "There are *some* perks to being a shape-shifter, you will see."

It was Wednesday morning, one of the three days a week that Rhianna Mori visited her grandfather at the nursing home. She usually joined him in his exercise routine and breakfast, but unlike him, she was not an early riser. He was worth it, of course, but it took effort to get her butt out of bed most days. And today was one of those days.

"Traffic?" he asked as she came through the door ten minutes late.

She smiled, knowing full well that he knew there wasn't much traffic in Auburn, Washington. "Sorry, Grandfather."

Shirō Mori stood near a large window, going through some Tai Chi moves.

She shed her jacket quickly and assumed her usual position alongside him.

Grandfather didn't miss a beat in his twenty-four form routine. His movements flowed from one move to the next without belying his ninety-six years. Rhia picked up where he was on form eight. She'd done this for so many years it was automatic.

They didn't speak again until the session was complete. Then he eased into his usual chair at the dinette table as she heated his traditional breakfast of Japanese tea, miso soup, and white rice in the microwave. "How are you today, Grandfather?"

"An old man."

She laughed. "Not so old."

He turned his face away and gazed out the window.

"What do you see?" she asked.

Still he stared off. "My journey."

She frowned and slid his food onto the table. "Here, this will give you strength."

He looked at her, and his gaze bore into her as if seeing deep inside her. "My time is growing near."

"You don't know that."

"Yes, I do. A man of my age can tell." He lifted the tea to his lips, sipped, and then set the cup back on the table.

"I only wish I knew what happened to my father. Then I could leave this world in peace."

She nibbled the corner of her lip. He'd said as much many times. The one thing he wanted before he passed was to find out what had happened to his father, her great-grandfather. As far as they knew, he'd just disappeared one day.

She wanted to know, too, and she had been working on it. She had been doing a lot of research, and there was a chance—an extremely slim chance—that she could get an all-expenses-paid trip to Japan where she could really learn more, maybe even find some evidence where her great-grandfather had been buried. She wanted so much to give her grandfather some closure before he died.

Of course, she'd have to go on a reality show to make it happen—as a Pilates instructor, she didn't exactly make big bucks—and her application was already in. Now all she had to do was wait and hope. While it's true she'd inherited a nice nest egg when her parents died in a plane crash years ago, that money was earmarked for her grandfather's care, and they were running out of it besides. Tears welled up in her eyes as she remembered the horror of that day. The devastation she had felt was never far from her mind. But she was thankful at least for the money that allowed her to give her grandfather the best care.

She placed her hand over his. If by some miracle she *was* selected to go on this journey, she needed to prepare her grandfather for her absence. They both knew his days were numbered, but she prayed he could hold on.

"You have something weighing on your mind, Child?"

"I may be traveling...to Japan."

He smiled. "This is wonderful."

"It's far from certain, but I should know in a few days. I just wanted to let you know in case I don't visit for a month or so."

He sucked in a breath. "A month?"

He glanced down to hide his disappointment, but she had already seen it in his eyes. "I probably won't get to go. I have to be chosen out of hundreds of applicants. And I don't even have to accept if they choose me. So don't worry. We can see how you are feeling and I can stay if you want me to."

"No. You mustn't hold up a magnificent opportunity such as this because of an old man. If it is your fate, it's your fate. It's not up to us." He pulled himself straighter.

She leaned over and kissed his cheek. "I love you, Grandfather."

Rhianna lifted out of plank position to discover a handsome, toned man standing in the doorway of her Pilates studio. Her business partner, Terri, wore a giddy smile as she stood beside him and waved Rhia over.

Rhianna tried not to groan. Terri knew Rhia hated stepping out on a class, and she was clearly in the middle of one. Couldn't they wait? Class was nearly over.

Terri waved more frantically.

Apparently not.

"Joy, will you lead the class in a cool down, please?" Rhia asked her assistant.

As Joy came to the front, Rhia headed to the back of the room. She redid the bobby pin holding her hair to the side while she walked, a little irritated. Ugh, she'd never get bangs again. Growing them out was such a pain.

She approached Terri and the stranger, and Terri tilted her head toward the exit. Rhia followed them out to the hallway with a sigh.

Her mind raced to fill in the blanks. The man looked vaguely familiar.

And that's when she noticed the cameraman.

What the…?

"Rhianna Mori?" the man asked with a practiced voice. "I'm Dillon Savage from the reality television show *If You Dare*, and you're our adventure-trip winner! So drop everything, and let's go!"

She stared at him, shocked and unprepared. She really hadn't thought she'd be chosen. But the surprise of it was sort of the point, wasn't it?

Another cameraman stepped into view off to her right. Here she was, in her exercise garb, and she was expected to drop what she was doing and take off for a dangerous, mysterious locale? In this case, the destination was Dragon's Vortex off the pacific coast of Japan, an area with more unexplainable incidents than the Bermuda Triangle. Planes and ships passed through that area and the people simply vanished, never to be heard from again.

Just like her great-grandfather.

Her heart thudded in her chest. Now was the time to back out if that's what she wanted to do.

No, You signed up for this, she reminded herself. She had to do it. She had to find out what exactly had happened to her great-grandfather, to at least try to come home with an answer that would give her grandfather peace.

For a few seconds, she numbly perused Dillon Savage. Funny, he was shorter than she'd expected and, while handsome, he wasn't nearly as appealing as he appeared on the clips she'd seen. The spontaneous thought caused her lips to tug to one side. He had cropped, curly, blond hair and was dressed fashionably in blue jeans and Ralph Lauren button-down.

Terri bounced on her toes and clapped, bringing Rhia back to the here and now. "This is so exciting." She grabbed hold of Rhia's shoulders and gave them a shake. "Go. Go. I'll take care of everything—your apartment, your plants, the business. I'll check in on your grandfather. Don't worry about a thing." She finished by wrapping her in a big hug.

Rhia squeezed her back, then stepped away, smoothing her hair with nervous fingers. She allowed her gaze to sweep back into the studio space, where Joy and the students were stealing glances toward the hallway. These people and her grandfather were all she had. It wouldn't be *that* bad if she never came back. It wasn't like she had a husband or children.

She lifted her chin, determined to see this through. She'd wanted to travel to Japan for so long, to not only find out about her great-grandfather's disappearance but to experience her heritage. Her ancestors on her father's side had been samurai warriors, and she'd traced her line back to the Nabekura Castle in northeastern Japan. And then...nothing.

But if she was honest with herself, those reasons were just part of why she'd signed up for the show six months ago. Now, more than ever, striking out on some outrageous adventure would do her good. She needed something new in her life, some excitement. She needed to prove to herself that she was strong and resourceful and her own person. Her ex-fiancé kept saying she couldn't make it without him. But he was wrong.

And if she peeled back her feelings further, she wanted to do something reckless for once in her life, like stare death in the face and having survival be all that mattered.

She shook her head. That's how much someone could crush you.

Then there was the million-dollar prize she'd win if she managed to return alive... That would certainly lift her worries about making her business work.

She took a deep breath. "Okay, Mr. Savage. Let's go."

He flashed his trademark smile. "Great! We must leave immediately," he said, following her to the entrance while the camera crew trailed behind.

"And we will. However, I believe I need my passport," she said with a wink. "Which is at home."

He laughed. "Ah yes. That's right."

She traipsed into the parking lot with Savage and the cameramen following behind her. Terri, Joy, and some of their students followed, too, and they hurried forward to line the walk.

"Be careful," Terri called out.

Rhianna raised a playful eyebrow. "Hey, I'm a second-degree black-belt. I know how to handle myself." She pulled her shoulders back. Before she'd moved to Auburn, she'd even volunteered at a college in Bellevue, teaching a women's self-defense class.

Terri tugged a hand through her hair. "Yeah, but still... Anything can happen."

"Have fun," one of her students shouted with a wave. The others joined in.

"I will!" She blew kisses to them with both hands and then slid into the back of the designated black SUV.

Her hands shook a little as she settled into the seat and watched her support group fade from view out the window, wondering if she'd ever see them again.

Aidan's stomach growled, and he glanced at his watch. *6:42.* He'd gotten home later than he'd expected and now was late for an inner tree meeting with his brothers. Crap.

He turned and hurried up to the main house, Takeshi at his heels. Moving through the kitchen, he grabbed a peach from the fruit bowl and exited into a passageway on the other side of the room, which led to the tree.

At the subterranean entrance to his Divine Tree, Aidan paused for acknowledgment of his inner tiger and eagle. A drop of sap penetrated his extended wrist in recognition, and he scooped up Takeshi as the tree allowed them entrance.

"Benison," Custos welcomed.

Aidan nodded. "Benison."

"Your brothers have been summoning you," the Divine Tree went on.

Aidan sighed. He wasn't used to rushing. There were few things that required urgency when one lived alone on an island. Still, he hurried to meet his brothers, heading down into the catacombs deep within the tree. Custos had already engaged his special link with the other ten trees throughout the world, each of the brothers appearing on a screen so the others could see him.

"It's about time," his brother Venn said when Aidan came into view of the group.

"Sorry to keep you waiting," Aidan apologized.

Ian, another of the Hearst brothers, chuckled. "Had your nose is some book, did you?"

Aidan had expected the ribbing. He, more than any of his brothers, enjoyed math, science, and philosophy. Which seemed strange since he was married to this island off the northeastern coast of Japan where his Divine Tree resided. But by studying every book he could get his hands on—and there were a lot with the age of computers—the world had opened to him.

He may be confined to an island, but it had all the comforts of any modern establishment, and then some. His *delegato* was his connection to the outside world, and he did a fine job of getting him everything he needed when he couldn't build it himself.

"I just returned from my journey to the mainland," Aidan explained.

"You left your tree unguarded?" Venn asked.

Aidan shrugged. Each of their Divine Trees was positioned in a special place with some near rare portholes into another universe, and as Guardians, they were to protect the trees of life from any intruders. He folded his arms over his chest. "There hasn't been anything happening here. No sign of anyone who shouldn't be here.

And things have been quiet with Theodora. I'm sure Custos would know if anything was up."

Venn pressed his lips together and shook his head slowly, clearly disappointed in Aidan. But they didn't understand what it was like to be all alone at all times.

Nonetheless, worry seeped into Aidan's chest. He swallowed. "What? Has there been action with you guys?"

"If you were *on time*, you'd know we've already been through that," Lachlan growled.

Aidan clenched his teeth. Had he known his brothers were going to be so testy, he might have skipped the meeting altogether.

Ian sighed. "There has been much going on in all the worlds, Brother. Even if there is no clear danger at present, it may be the calm before the storm. With the Age of Atonement—"

"I know," Aidan interrupted. "We must be diligent."

"So then why were you traveling to the mainland?" Ian inquired.

Takeshi barked, as if he knew Aidan was about to mention him.

Brandt's mug came closer to one of the screens, filling the entire thing. "What was that? Did you get a new pup?"

Aidan smiled as his brother's all leaned toward their screens. "That's why I was on the mainland."

"What breed?" Lachlan asked, his earlier frustration falling from his voice. Then they all started asking him questions. They knew how hard Aidan had taken the loss of Sora, and it meant a lot that they were trying.

"Akita," Aidan answered, picking up Takeshi again and showing them.

"Uh, umm, very cute." Ian cleared his throat. "Now can we get back to our meeting?"

Takeshi barked again and wriggled out of Aidan's arms, only to start pulling on the leg of his pants. Aidan laughed and then shrugged.

"I guess that's a no," Ian said, resigned. "Well, keep your eyes open and reach out should anything change."

"I will," Aidan promised. "Be careful, Brothers."

They each nodded in turn, and Custos disconnected them one after the other.

"Now," Custos grumbled, "get that creature out of my tree."

2

Rhianna braced herself against the onslaught of the next gust of wind that beat against the helicopter. It had been two days since she'd left the States, and now they were flying to the deserted island of Tsuriairando, in the heart of the Dragon Vortex.

"Be ready," Hedai, the chopper pilot said over his shoulder. "I want to get in and get the hell out. These haunted waters are cursed."

"That's what all the locals have told me," she admitted. The reason for their unease was clear: no one traveled willingly to this area. Too many people didn't come back.

"Because it is true, Miss," he said.

Suddenly the helicopter pitched off its mark by several feet. The pilot swore in Japanese and circled around, making adjustments on the descent. Below, the waves slapped against the sandbar that jutted off the south end of the island. She was to be dropped off here. Evidently, it was the only section of solid ground devoid of trees and dense vegetation.

"Are you sure you want to head out today? Can you handle the weather?" asked the chopper's copilot, Steve, seeming far more concerned about her welfare than the TV show's director and host had been.

She flicked a glance at Savage, who was sitting beside her. "I'll be fine," she answered, adjusting the waterproof GoPro on her head. The camera and a satellite telephone would be her only connection to the team and the outside world once they dropped her off. She inhaled deeply, her heart tripping in her chest.

Three weeks. Alone. To discover if the boogeyman actually existed in the Dragon Vortex.

Savage placed a firm hand on her shoulder. "People will tune in and watch because they want to feel connected; they want to be there. They want to feel what it's like to be on an island, alone, in a place where so many have died." He squeezed her shoulder harder. "Give them a good show."

She nodded, the nervousness growing in her stomach.

The helicopter wobbled from left to right as it descended farther. Rhianna clenched her hands into fists, anticipating the touchdown; she wished she could see out the door. At least then she'd know how close they were. Finally, the landing skids settled lightly onto the sand, and the sinking feeling in her stomach let up. She exhaled a sigh of relief. That was far more controlled than she'd expected.

Steve slid open the side door of the helicopter. The wind came rushing in, striking her face and whipping her hair out of the bobby pin it had been secured with. When she swiped her hair away and resecured it, she got her first view of the island.

Swiss Family Robinson come to life. It reminded her a little of New Zealand. She'd like to go there someday, too…if she survived this.

Savage slid to the edge to help her out—and so he'd be in view of the camera.

"Okay. Out you go," he said.

Her heart hammered faster, but she chased any doubts from her mind. She scooted to the edge of the chopper and quickly climbed out. Her feet sank into the sand as water gushed across her shins in waves, exacerbated by the helicopter's gusts.

Savage thrust a canvas supply satchel toward her. "Here's your survival bag."

Her arm sagged as she accepted it. "My goodness, it's heavy."

"It includes the extra batteries for your electronics and a solar recharger, so keep those dry in the waterproof bag," he ordered. "You won't get any replacements, so take care of them. And you'll need to ration your food."

She nodded. Another wave of apprehension washed over her. Man, she hadn't recalled those details from the briefing. What else had she missed?

As he dipped back inside the chopper, Savage yelled, "Oh, and remember, if you need help, you can contact us via the Sat phone. We'll be stationed on the yacht not far away but, you know, out of the danger zone. We should get your GoPro video via Livestream." He gave her a thumbs-up.

She returned the gesture, indicating she was all set.

Then she ducked her head and hustled away from the chopper, following the sandbar. When she was clear, she stopped and glanced back. It rose and flew away. She stood transfixed, watching it disappear out to sea.

Even through the whir of the wind, she could hear her heartbeat thudding in her ears. She swallowed hard.

Too late for second thoughts, Rhia.

The program was more of a reality-show expedition about why people disappeared than a show that would *actually* allow her to die, she reminded herself. She would be one of the few who *did* make it out of the Dragon Vortex.

Eventually, she noticed the lap of the surf against her legs. The waves were rough, sending sets of whitecaps rolling over the sandbar. She turned and tromped along the sand to the shore, her running shoes creating a sucking *kerplop* with every step.

Reaching the shore, she took stock of her location. From this vantage point, the sandbar was easy to spot, but judging from the dense vegetation up and down the coastline, she doubted that would be the case when she was traveling from the opposite direction, from the inland out. She'd have to remember that when she was making her way back here to be picked up when the twenty-one days were over.

She chewed her lower lip. The sky was full of nasty-looking clouds, making it impossible to determine the placement of the sun to get her bearings.

She couldn't help but wonder if visibility had anything to do with why the victims went missing.

Takeshi's bark engaged the sound-activated alarm clock, which automatically set off the machinations of the morning. The vibration of the drum triggered a rise of a lever, sending a metal ball rolling along a track until it knocked a swinging gate against a switch that filled a coffeepot with water, then an arm set it on the stove. And so it went, like a finely tuned assembly line.

As he got out of bed, washed his face, dressed and traipsed into the kitchen, the rhythm of clicks and clacks of moving objects created a backdrop and illusion of being busy. The sort of noise one really didn't have when living alone on a deserted island. But the system he'd created filled that void.

It wasn't the same as having someone to snuggle with when he woke up in the morning, of course. And Takeshi traipsing across the bed certainly didn't count.

Aidan slid a fried egg from a pan onto a plate and gave a second one to the dog. "Hmm, I seem to be getting up earlier since you arrived," he grumbled to Takeshi. He hadn't realized how laid-back he'd become with the pup's predecessor.

His lifestyle allowed for total flexibility. He spent his days inventing things and tinkering with machines. Just last night he'd been working with a piece of copper, honing it to create a funnel to help channel more water from the waterfall into the turbine to generate electricity at a higher rate. His home on the island had to be self-sufficient after all, being that it was so remote. His *delegato* also presented his inventions to the world, which earned Aidan sufficient income to expand his innovations and interests.

After he'd eaten, he climbed the staircase from his living quarters to the aboveground solarium. It was situated on the peak of a mountainous rise from which he could see both sides of the island on a clear day, plus the canopy of the sacred oak tucked in the valley below. He inhaled a deep breath, gazing out the windows, and frowned at the fog enveloping the island.

"It will clear," he predicted to Takeshi. "Come, I'll show you the island."

The pup lifted his chin, his tail wagging like the blade of a mixer, and followed as Aidan led the way to an outer deck. He decided to introduce his tiger form to begin with so he could stay close to the pup. The eagle would come later.

Takeshi sat very still as Aidan changed from man to cat, tilting his head as if not quite sure what to make of the transition. When Aidan strode closer, the pup jumped back with a yip. Takeshi darted left and then right. Aidan slowly circled around him, and then initiated a game of back-and-forth play. Soon the pup was trotting between Aidan's strong, powerful legs, weaving around and brushing up against him, his curiosity clearly outweighing his fear.

When Aidan thought the connection was strong enough for the pup to stay with him, he led the way down the mountain and into the thick forest. *Come,* he instructed with his mind. *Let's be free.*

Rhianna gave a huge sigh as she took in the thick foliage. Everywhere she looked, there were trees. The reality was a little daunting for a city girl who had gone on only a handful of outdoors excursions, all of which had been in her college days. Washington had tall, stately trees, but none of the places she'd visited shared this thick, wild growth. Her parents had been the types to save everything they earned, so taking extravagant vacations had been out of the question as a child, even though they lived in one of the most gorgeous states on the planet.

Knowing she had to find shelter before the rain started, Rhianna found an opening in the enormous, tightly packed trees. She picked her way through and found that there were several open areas where she could make camp. Later, she would explore and find a more permanent spot for a home base, but for tonight, she chose a group of fallen trees near a wide, overhanging ledge.

She was preparing to take a closer look when a dog's bark ripped through the wind. She turned toward the sound but saw no one. She could have sworn it had been a dog...

She flinched as her satellite phone rang. She pulled it from the satchel and answered it. "Rhia here."

"Hi, sweetheart," Savage's sugary voice greeted her. "Just double-checking the equipment."

"It's working. Thanks," she said, grateful that he was checking on her.

"Good. Good. Then I'll—"

"Savage, wait," she interrupted.

"Yes?"

"This island is supposed to be uninhabited, right?"

"That's right."

She paused as she considered telling him about the dog she'd heard, but then thought better of it. When she had researched animals on the islands, there had been no mention of dogs, but that didn't mean there couldn't be wild dogs or some other animal. And she didn't want to seem like a wuss less than thirty minutes after landing.

"Well, good luck," he said before the phone went silent.

"Thanks," she whispered to herself, then clicked the "off" button.

Another dog bark echoed in her ears. This time she was sure of it. *They have to be wild,* she thought with a shiver. *And probably hungry.*

Slinging the backpack over one shoulder, she trudged deeper into the tree line and up beneath the ledge she'd found earlier. She dropped the pack with a heavy sigh. "Not hauling that sucker around any great distance," she mumbled.

It was medium size, like the ones people used for mountain climbing, orange on top and dark gray on the bottom, with a few side pockets. It might not have looked like it, but it weighed a ton. She checked the side pockets and found a lighter, knife with a sheath, and a small flashlight. The latter she'd have to use sparingly. She wondered if they'd included extra batteries for that, too. Turning on the beam of light, she opened her pack and searched through it. The additional GoPro equipment was on top, and she quickly located the solar charger and batteries, including some smaller wattages.

Rummaging deeper revealed some meal bars and a few bottles of water—those weren't going to last long. At the very bottom, her hand struck something hard and metal. She wrapped her hand around it and pulled it out. Her breath caught when she saw what it was.

A gun? Why would she need a gun?

Okay, the producers obviously knew this would be a dangerous expedition. The premise of the show revolved around the idea that she might come face-to-face with whatever was responsible for so many people vanishing, never to be heard from again.

A rumble of thunder sounded, and she glanced around at the growing dark clouds. First things first, she had to build some shelter or else she'd be drenched. She shoved everything back into the backpack except for the knife.

Rhia worked a circle outward as she gathered sticks and branches. She brought them beneath the rock shelter. When she'd accumulated a pile about four feet high, she pulled the knife from its sheath, cut the longer branches down to usable campfire-sized pieces, and assembled them into the shape of a teepee. Even though she hadn't had much personal experience in the wild, she'd seen enough television programs to know what she needed to do.

But it wasn't quick—or easy. The leaves and branches were damp and didn't catch fire right away. She tried over and over and over. At this rate the lighter would soon be useless. In every survival program she'd ever watched, they'd pounded home the necessity of a fire: to boil clean water, to keep warm, to ward off predators.

She thought of the dog she'd heard earlier and redoubled her effort.

Finally, a leaf caught. And then another and another. She sat back on her heels. *Yes!*

She inhaled and exhaled in a rush of excitement. She'd done it! Whew.

Carefully, she added more kindling to the fire. As she watched it burn, she realized just how much wood it would take to keep it going. At this rate, all she'd be doing the entire month was collecting wood. That wouldn't work.

She needed time to meditate and tap into the energy and spirit that was her great-grandfather. Then, given a closer proximity to where he'd disappeared, perhaps she would discover his fate.

On her next wood scavenging trip, she found a long, straight stick that would make for a decent spear in case she needed protection. She took it back to camp. The question was, did she have what it took to use it if the time came? Or the gun, for that matter…

In his tiger form, Aidan halted well within the dense forest and listened. A woman's voice floated to him on the rustle of tree branches. Alarm slammed into his chest, humans on his island never turned out well.

He growled softly to Takeshi, who paused several yards beyond Aidan and also raised his ears.

What on earth was a female doing on his island?

Aidan shooed the pup in the opposite direction. He wanted to move in for a closer look at the woman, yet at the same time, he couldn't risk the pup darting out and becoming friendly. On a sigh, he transformed into his human body and scooped Takeshi into the crook of his arm. Yes. The best plan would be to remain hidden until she left.

The pup yipped.

"No." Aidan whispered the command.

"There are not supposed to be dogs inhabiting this island." Her voice held a pleasant tone, not really fearful but not sure of herself, either. She seemed to be trying to convince herself that she'd just been hearing things.

Takeshi wiggled to get free, and Aidan stroked the pup from head to haunches. "Sorry, I can't put you down." His stomach clinched. He was wary of this woman.

Needing to know more, Aidan worked his way through the shrubs until he achieved a partially unobstructed view. He cautiously peered between the greenery, ready to dart back at any second. Takeshi must have read his hesitant stance, for the pup grew still.

The female stepped from the foliage and stood in profile, with one hand on her hip, the other holding a large walking stick as she gazed out to sea. Her scent drifted to him, and he inhaled a long, appreciative whiff. She smelled of cinnamon and spices mixed with her own sweet fragrance.

She was the only new fragrance he detected, though. Which confirmed she was out here all alone. But why?

Her hair was the color of mahogany and barely touched her shoulders; it was actually much shorter than his own. She wore a camera strapped across her forehead, and she sported exercise clothes—form-fitting pants that hugged her legs to her calves and a tank top of black, peach, and sea green swirls.

Was she an adventurer of some sort? He'd seen the helicopter fly over a short while ago, yet he couldn't fathom why anyone would drop her off *here*. To the world, this was an uninhabited island. One where people disappeared. The Japanese natives were very superstitious about the island, creating tales of dragons, hence the name Dragon Vortex.

He watched as she gathered sticks and branches for a stockpile of firewood. Her graceful movements were intriguing. He had few opportunities to observe people, or interact with anyone for that matter, except when he did so via computer. A yearning stirred inside him as she went about her tasks. The sway of her hips, the reach of her willowy arm, the angle of her chin as she seemed to consider her next choice… Liquid heat spread through him.

Without warning, Takeshi slipped through his grasp, launched from his arms, and bolted in her direction. *Dammit.* He lunged forward several steps and stopped short of revealing himself as Takeshi entered her camp.

The female's head snapped up. She froze, studying the

pup, and her eyes grew round with alarm even as a smile pulled the corners of her mouth upward. "I knew I heard a dog."

Without hesitation, Takeshi bounded over to her.

She gasped and drew back several steps. "Are you wild?"

But the pup simply sat at her feet and then sprawled on his belly.

She observed him for a few more seconds. She knelt, then stretched her arm out, presenting the back of her hand to him. "Why, you're just a puppy. How did you get here?"

Takeshi rose and nuzzled the woman's hand.

Traitor.

Aidan retreated farther into the shadows. He couldn't possibly get his dog back without revealing himself. He sighed. The goal was to get the woman to leave without discovering the Divine Tree. But he'd also have to wait until the pup decided to return to its owner.

The dog pushed his way onto her lap. She sat back on her bottom and crossed her legs, laughing. It was a delightful sound—warm, inviting, gentle. In all his loneliness, it was definitely a sound he could get used to.

But why is she here? he asked himself again. His brother Ian's words rang back in his ears: *Even if there is no clear danger at present, it may be the calm before the storm.*

He clenched his teeth. Could this female be part of that coming storm? Or the cause of it?

She reached up and flicked on the camera. "Look what I found. I thought I'd heard a dog barking earlier. He's such a sweetie."

Why was she filming here? Who was she speaking to? The camera made him uneasy...as if the secrets of the island were going to be revealed.

With a warning flaring inside him, he went into protection mode as he transformed into his eagle.

3

His arms morphed into powerful wings that caught the current of air and lifted him off the ground. The rest of his body changed at the same time, and he could feel the tiny pinpricks of feathers forming, not actually painful but perceptible. The process was seamless, and it was natural for him now, although it wasn't always so. In the beginning, he had to learn how to fly like any baby bird. Trial and error had been a bitch.

He dug his talons into the ground to gain purchase before he launched into the air. As he did so, the earth shook with a vibration he felt deep in his bones.

Aw, shit. That isn't good.

His whole body was suddenly alert and on guard. If his guess was correct, someone had just broken through from the Riam dimension. And that someone was probably the sorceress, Theodora. Depending on her intent and mood, the experience ranged from a minor earthquake tremor to a sonic boom.

She'd taunted him in the past, trying to persuade him to give up secrets from the Divine Tree. Now she would want this woman. He was sure of it…just as she desired all humans who passed through the Dragon Vortex.

He tensed. In every instance when someone had visited the island, sorceress Theodora had taken them to her alternate universe, Riam. He didn't actually know what the place looked like, for no person who had ever been here left again. As far as he knew, the only way in or out of Riam was through Theodora. Custos had told him it was a place of continuous fighting and the people she took there became warriors.

Aidan flew in a high circle over the woman and the pup. Neither paid any attention to him.

If Theodora was visiting his island, experience told him it was the woman who drew her here. As he banked, his gaze swept the area. The sorceress materialized from the mist shrouding the trees. Slowly, she descended to the ground. Her long black dress hung in strips around her ankles, however, the bodice fit perfectly to her body.

Fear for the woman's safety struck him hard. Theodora was a mix breed of siren and Valkyrie who had been given the gift of magic from the Demon Prince, and she was like a dog sniffing out a bone when it came to visitors to the Dragon Vortex. The chilling sorceress hadn't wasted any time seeking out the female, either. Maybe it was simply coincidence, or maybe with the approaching Age of Atonement, she'd been waiting for an opportunity. For what, he didn't know. Another go at trying to get knowledge from the Divine Tree, perhaps? He had stopped her last time, but not without Custos' help.

An odd expression crossed Theodora's face as she paused, seeming to admire her surroundings. He wondered what went through her malicious mind. Her features relaxed and her eyes shone florescent green. Something seemed to hold her in check, as if she were testing the waters. Could that be because she knew he was watching?

Aidan flew to a branch where he could see both the female and the sorceress, although it would be like watching a tennis match if he had to turn from one to the other.

A snap of a twig alerted him someone was on the move and he jerked his gaze to the woman. She was walking through the trees, Takeshi close behind her. Suddenly she paused, talking as if to herself. But then she took the portable camera from her brow and turned it toward herself, and he realized she was documenting her actions for some reason.

"It's day one here in the Dragon Vortex, and I've settled in at my overnight location. The fire is going—" she looked up at the impending storm "—but I'm not sure how long it will last. I'll probably get rained out any second. And as you can see, I have an unexpected friend." She reached down and stroked the pup's head.

On the heel of her words, large drops began to fall from the sky. A few intermittent splotches at first, and then the rain started to come down faster, each plop a little smaller and more intense than the ones before. She ducked beneath the ledge, curling her limbs in under the cover of the rock. "And that's it for now. Rhianna Mori signing off from day one of *On Your Own* in the Pacific Ocean."

So that was her name. *Rhianna*. He tossed it around in his thoughts, liking the sound. Pretty, like her.

But the rest of what she'd said was beyond him.

Theodora strolled right into Rhianna's camp, halting a few feet away from him. Rhianna didn't so much as shift her gaze. She just stared straight ahead.

Aidan tensed. Theodora was invisible to humans unless she chose to reveal herself. One of her many sorcery powers. And she usually only revealed herself when she was going to do something horrible. He had to get her to leave before she did something irreversible.

It's been awhile, Aidan said, mentally transferring the conversation to her.

Yes. Now what have we here? she asked.

Go back to your world, Theodora.

She turned her head to look at him and smiled wickedly. With a raised eyebrow, she asked, *Now why would I want to do that?*

It was verbal play, he knew; she didn't truly want an answer.

She doesn't know anything about our worlds, he said roughly. *Let her be in hers.*

Perhaps.

She was taunting him. Theodora loved to play games…and change rules. The encounters he'd had with her over the centuries left him with a lot of uncertainties. To his understanding, according to Custos, the people who she'd taken by force into her alternate universe were not dead, nor completely alive, but somehow they simply existed. She kept them as her pets. *Or more like entertainment.* But the truth was, he'd never been to Riam, so he wasn't certain.

He only sensed he didn't want Theodora to capture this woman.

Rhianna placed the recording equipment inside a bag—he hoped it was waterproof—and then unwrapped some sort of snack bar and ate. Eyeing Takeshi, she broke off a piece and fed it to him. "What do you eat out here? How do you survive?" she asked softly. There was a fresh innocence about her that made his chest flutter. He tried to shake off the feeling. He couldn't be drawn in, couldn't care. He just needed to send her on her way.

But something within him resisted. As ridiculous as it seemed, he felt something for this woman. Maybe it was her beauty, or the fact that all the other humans who had come to the island had been men. Maybe it was protectiveness that stirred inside him at knowing if

Theodora took this woman, he couldn't leave his tree and venture after them.

An unfamiliar restlessness tugged at him. He stared at Rhianna as she made a bed of palm branches. She looked up at the limb where he was perching and spotted his eagle. Their gazes held.

Oh, how sweet, Theodora commented. *I think you like her.*

Irritation flared that she'd read his feelings so easily. He *did* like this woman, this Rhianna. He would not admit it to Theodora, though.

Now that Rhianna had noticed him, he decided to move a little closer. He flew to a lower branch across the clearing, putting himself between her and the sorceress.

He didn't think Theodora would try anything yet. Straight and to the point was not her style. She liked to drag it out, to get the most entertainment value from it as she could.

That was a good thing this time. It would give him more opportunity to come up with a plan and outsmart her.

From past encounters, he'd gleaned that she trolled the Pacific, its islands and waters, and collected her victims. She was the reason the Dragon Vortex had gotten its reputation. Because the people who entered this area were not only lost but usually not in this dimension any longer.

Rhianna patted a spot on her makeshift bed. "Come on," she said to the dog. "It's dry in here."

Takeshi trotted beneath the shelter and curled up next to her.

Hmph. Theodora snorted. Abruptly, she cocked her chin and looked off to the side, as if tuning in to something else, something far beyond even his enhanced hearing. She snapped her head back to glare at him. *I'll be back*—she pointed a finger at him—*and then you're going to give me this sweet girl on a silver platter.*

With that, Theodora disappeared.

Aidan took a deep breath and returned his attention to

Rhianna, only to find her watching him with apprehension. Then she flicked both hands at him. "Go away. Shoo," she said. "You're making me nervous."

He angled his head at her. Nervousness was the least of her problems.

"I'm sure those claws are sharp," she mumbled. "I wish I recalled if eagles attack humans…"

He could if he wanted to. But if the eagle bothered her, he wondered what she'd think of his tiger. Perhaps if he showed her that form, she'd be scared enough to call someone to come get her.

Given the mountainous terrain behind them, the sun disappeared quickly, leaving behind a sudden drop in temperature along with the darkness. She still had that fire going, but it wouldn't last through the night, even with the firewood she'd gathered. And it got very cold out here in the elements.

He *could* change into a human and take her to his home. But she'd probably have a heart attack at that. Instead, he decided to run to the Divine Tree where he had a sleeping bag stored. He'd set it where she'd discover it.

The plan appealed to him. He liked the idea of helping her, but he knew he couldn't leave her for long in case Theodora returned. So he would have to be quick.

After that, he would hunker down for the night and watch over her.

Rhianna's back muscles loosened, and she let out a sigh of relief as the eagle flew off.

Good. It was gone.

The rain had eased to a misty drizzle. She zipped her jacket up beneath her chin and then rubbed her hands up and down her arms. She was pretty sure the show's producers hadn't been so nice as to include chemical hand warmers or any such thing in her emergency kit, but she'd check anyway.

She clicked on her flashlight and dug to the bottom of the sack. The light reflected off something, and she reached in and removed the item. It was a Mylar thermal blanket. She hadn't noticed it when she'd looked earlier. She grinned from ear to ear at the find. She wouldn't have to worry so much about the fire now. This would at least keep her fairly warm and dry.

The Mylar made a crinkling sound as she opened the package and unfolded the blanket. She wrapped it around her shoulders and snuggled back into her sheltered spot. This would do for tonight. Tomorrow she'd have to find the perfect place to call home for the next twenty-one days. Someplace dry, out of the wind, and with access to fresh water.

Closing her eyes, she sighed. A warmth formed in her core and spread outward into her limbs.

Mmm. Much better.

She couldn't shake the feeling of being watched, though, as she stared out into the darkness beyond the firelight. Her vision darted around from one black spot to another. The puppy snuggled up to her hip, comforting her.

After being awake for what seemed like hours, she finally fell into a restless sleep. At one point, she thought the night would never end, she'd awoken so many times. But eventually, the sky grew lighter, the first hint of dawn bathing the sky in a soft lavender and then pink. The hues were quite muted and hazy given the mist that shrouded the island, but as the sun rose, a brightness filled on the horizon.

Rhianna sat up, pressing her back against the dirt wall behind her. She wasn't in any hurry to get up and leave her warm cocoon. She had all day to accomplish the next step and explore the area. If she found some artifacts, they may give a clue about other people who had stumbled onto the island.

She glanced to where the eagle had been yesterday. The spot was empty. Then her gaze swept the trees and surrounding area to see if it had moved, but she couldn't find it.

She stood slowly, keeping the crinkling blanket wrapped around her as best she could, and moved to the nearly extinguished fire. Goodness that Mylar was loud! At least any nearby wild creature would hear her and stay away. But not the pup; he followed at her heels.

She decided the best way to warm up was to do some morning exercises, just like she did at home. She set the Mylar blanket aside and strolled to the beach, the dog walking right along with her. The cove of the island faced southeast, and in the fog-kissed sunrise, she went through her Tai Chi sequence. The stretches felt so good after the long hours of traveling she'd done the past few days. As she bent over to touch the ground again, the dog ran up to her and licked her face and neck, making her laugh and nearly fall over.

When she finished, she headed back to the fire. She'd need to stoke it and get it roaring again. She stirred the ashes with a stick. In the middle, the coals flared red.

The pup stuck his nose close to the embers. "No," she commanded. "It's hot."

The dog quickly stepped back. "Oh, you're a smart one, aren't you?" she asked with a laugh. "You stay back while I work, okay?"

The pup barked as if in answer.

She went over to the stockpile of kindling and branches she'd stored beneath the ledge and grabbed some leaves and sticks. She layered them over the glowing embers and then leaned closer to lightly blow on them until a fire sparked. When it flamed, she carefully placed larger sticks and branches one on top of the other. The fire climbed along the dry wood.

Satisfied, she warmed her hands near the heat. God, it

felt good. According to her research, this area maintained a temperature between forty and seventy degrees in October. This morning definitely felt like the lower end of that spectrum. And according to Google, it rained seventeen out of thirty days. Traveling inland to find a permanent dry shelter was definitely at the top of her to-do list today.

Reluctantly leaving the fire, she headed for the firewood she'd stored beneath the ridge. Taking a few steps in that direction she froze in mid-stride. What? There was a sleeping bag resting next to the pile of broken branches she'd gathered last night.

How did it get there?

She searched the surrounding area. Had someone from the reality show crew delivered it during the night? That seemed a bit farfetched given the premise of the show, yet she didn't have another explanation.

A chill ran through her, one that had nothing to do with the biting wind. Someone had entered her camp and she hadn't even realized it.

From the deep shadows of the trees, Aidan watched in his tiger form. She'd found the sleeping bag he'd left. At least she'd have something more than that noisy Mylar to keep her warm tonight. That is, if he hadn't convinced her to go home by then.

She grabbed the GoPro from her satchel and put it on, this time using a chest harness. She spoke to her presumed audience. "Good morning, everyone. Welcome to day two of *If You Dare*. I'm here in what the locals call the Dragon Vortex, which covers about 600,000 square miles off the coast of northern Japan, with this deserted island situated smack-dab in the middle. This is the island of Tsuriairando, which means 'tree island.'"—she swept her arms left and right—"for obvious reasons."

Aidan stretched his spine. Yes, she seemed to be documenting her journey for some reason, walking around and capturing the island on camera.

"The legend goes that a dragon resides in this area and eats anyone who ventures here. Which is the local's explanation as to why hundreds of people have vanished in this area, never to be heard from again. Planes have crashed; ships have been found abandoned."

She crouched nearer to the fire, warming her hands. She pursed her lips and paused in thought. The adorable expression touched something in him, called to him, and made him want to help her even more.

"So, here I am," she continued, "daring to defy the odds of surviving the unknown. I'll let you know if I see any such mythical creatures." She peered at Takeshi. "And this little guy doesn't count, even though there supposedly aren't any domestic animals on this island. That obviously isn't the case," she said, twisting her lips into a smile.

He liked listening to her. It was like the sun rising on the water, vibrant yet quiet and smooth, with a hint of an accent. And since he was the only one here, it felt like she was speaking directly to him.

"Okay," she said, grabbing the pan from the pack and glancing at Takeshi. "Let's head down to the ocean and see if I can rustle up some clams for breakfast."

She walked toward the water carrying a knife, a tall walking stick, and the pan. After she'd passed by him, still in tiger form, he slowly moved from his hiding place and lumbered after her, keeping his distance.

Show yourself. Frighten her so she will flee the island and not return.

He knew that was his best chance to get her to leave. But it wasn't as simple as it sounded. What if she caught him on her camera?

At the water's edge, she squatted and dug the knife in the sand. It didn't take long for her to unearth a couple of fist-sized clams. The island was rich with them, so he wasn't surprised how quickly she found some, but she obviously didn't know that and started jumping up and down, holding the clams in front of the camera.

"Look! Look. I did it!" She laughed, then set them in the pan.

Aidan stepped back into the shadows, to make sure she wouldn't see him. He gave a feline smile. He enjoyed watching her; she was so sweet and seemingly naive in a good way. Rhianna skipped right past him again, this time with her prize.

After a moment, he followed her once more, staying hidden. Just a little longer, and then he'd frighten her and send her on her way.

Back at her makeshift camp, she took the camera and placed it on a stand to the side of the fire, facing toward her. Then she found a medium-sized rock and, using some sticks, repositioned the firewood. She set the rock in the middle of the fire, placing the clams on it, and positioned the burning wood and embers around it. She stood, resting a hand on her hip and looking into the camera.

"I'm not sure if this will work, but here's hoping." She crossed her fingers, held them up, and smiled. "Dillion? What do ya think? I get an A, huh?" she asked into the camera as her hair did a bouncy swish.

Aidan groaned in appreciation as he sat back on his haunches and waited. He really didn't have enough human contact, he thought. That must be the reason for the anxious flutter against his ribs.

While the clams cooked, she hummed to herself as she tried to fold the Mylar blanket without much success. Myriad emotions from frustration to acceptance crossed her face as she struggled with the noisy material. Finally, she thrust the disheveled bundle aside.

She turned to the camera and pointed at the blanket. "Just a side note, those are *not* meant to be folded back up." She shrugged, walking back to the fire. "I'll just be using it again tonight anyway."

She grabbed a pair of sticks and used them to lift the clams from the fire. Next she reached inside her backpack and pulled out a canteen of water. "This is the last of the water I was provided. I'll have to find a fresh water source today and replenish it."

Aidan liked the way she talked to the camera. He was getting to know her, just as her audience was. Too bad it had to all end soon.

Taking a couple of other rocks with her, Rhianna sat near the fire. She tried to lift one of the clams, only to shake her fingers and hiss in a breath of air. "Whoa. Hot."

Aidan stood, stretching out his front paws and back, as she picked up her knife and stared at it. He wondered if she really knew how to use it without cutting off her fingers. He paced. Dammit, he had no confidence in a woman wielding a knife with such uncertainty.

With an abrupt glint of light off the blade, the sudden image of his mother surfaced in his memory. His mum had been an expert in the kitchen. It had been so so long since she'd been alive. She had been a solid Scottish woman with long curly hair, which she usually braided into a plait and wound on top of her head.

He sighed. No, perhaps his appraisal of this woman was wrong.

Assessing the problem, she searched the area, coming back with a rock to use as a cutting board. She knelt and pressed the edge of the blade on one of the clams, trying to pry it open. The clam rolled to the side, and the knife nicked the rock with a *chink*. She tried again. And again. And again.

On the fifth attempt, the tip of the blade held and split the clam. "Finally," she said with a relieved exhale. She grinned down at Takeshi. "I did it."

Her look of satisfaction was contagious, and he was

happy for her. Unfortunately, her delight would dissolve in a minute when he showed himself. What would it hurt to allow her to savor her victory for a moment, though?

As he watched, he tamped down the mushy feeling inside that threatened to weaken him. Ignoring the sensation, he drew himself taller and assumed his full tiger stance, which proved to be at least twice the size of an average tiger given his Guardian influences. Navigating from within the brush, he advanced toward her in slow, controlled steps.

Her head snapped up as he came into view, and she screamed. She scrambled to her feet. The look of fear in her eyes as her jaw fell open made his chest hurt—precisely where he'd experienced that warm flurry of sensation moments earlier. However, his feelings didn't matter. He had to get her to leave in order to save her life. To that end, he roared at her, flashing his teeth in a long, forceful exhale.

She jumped. And he could hear her heart pounding faster, wildly out of control. Her eyes widened as she stared at him, frozen in place. Takeshi darted between them and snarled, baring his teeth.

Oh great. The pup was standing up to his owner to protect Rhianna.

She slowly backed up to the backpack and dug inside. She pulled out a gun, pointed it at him, and disengaged the safety. Her hands trembled as she aimed, her jaw set in clear determination. Then she walked sideways, watching him the entire time.

Aidan continued to progress, narrowing the distance between them. Her gaze shot to the camera, which he belatedly realized was still filming. He couldn't decide if that was good or bad. He hoped when her friends saw the footage, they'd come to her rescue. He only hoped they would leave it at that and let him be.

"Go away," she said to him as he neared.

Her weight shifted. She was going to shoot!

As the bullet flew from the gun, he jumped high and to the side. Even with his evasive action, the shot hit his thigh, eliciting a fiery pain just above his knee.

He heard her quick steps, muffled by the thud of his paws against the earth as he landed. She dashed over to the camera and unhooked it from the stand. With a flick of her wrist, she aimed the camera at him.

She mumbled, her words rapid-fire, "You're going to ruin everything. Go back to your den. Just go."

He had no idea what she meant or why she was reacting so oddly, but the only thing he was going to ruin was her chance at being kidnapped—and possibly *killed*—by Theodora.

Rhianna brushed the back of her hand at him and then froze, as if waiting for him to comply. He didn't, of course.

He stalked forward, ignoring the pain in his leg. She went on alert and eased backward. The rhythm they set was like a sophisticated dance, testing each other's resolve. She pulled her shoulders back and took a formidable stance. He had the feeling she wouldn't back down easily, and when they reached a large tree, she slid behind it.

Was she trying to hide, just hoping he would go away? If he were an average tiger, he would have sunk his teeth into her by now. He roared, then paused, thinking she was holding her breath, that she was standing perfectly still and listening for his movements the same way he was listening for hers. Expelling tension along with the air in his lungs, he decided to give her a chance—one chance—to call her team to get her the hell out of here. And if she didn't...well, the consequences would be entirely her fault.

With that thought, a stabbing pain shot up his leg into his back. The bullet must have struck a nerve. The agony was so intense, he dropped to the ground and immediately returned to his human form.

A loud thumping drummed in her head. Her own heartbeat, she realized, as she plastered her spine against the tree trunk. Her stomach churned. The tiger hadn't followed her. Good. She concentrated on slowing her breathing and controlling her anxiety.

Darn it, she didn't know what she'd expected to discover in the Dragon Vortex. Her great-grandfather had disappeared here over a hundred years ago. There wouldn't be any clues or records as to how or why he had never returned, but she'd spoken with the locals prior to coming here. Plus, if he had been on the island his essence may remain. It wasn't unheard of for a person's imprint to remain on objects they'd touched.

Her palms grew moist. She was in over her head, and she knew it. She'd never before attempted a spiritual connection this advanced.

So why was she really here? She'd felt a calling like she'd never experienced, a need to give her grandfather some sort of answer before he died. That's why.

With another deep breath, she peered around the tree. The tiger was gone. For several seconds, she collapsed against the tree in relief. When her stomach had calmed, she turned the camera toward her. "Did you see that? There's a tiger on this island. A friggin' tiger. If I go dark, then you better start looking for my bones."

Cautiously, she stepped away from the tree and moved closer to her camp. She gasped. Precisely where the gigantic tiger had been, a man was lying on his back. Blood oozed from a leg wound, soaking his jeans.

OMG. How on earth did he get there? And where did the tiger go?

She hesitated. The man had to have come from somewhere. But where? And how had he gotten injured?

Her stomach dropped. She hadn't accidentally shot him somehow, had she?

The puppy ran straight to the man and licked his face.

Her stomach tightened as she watched the interaction. Something didn't seem right. Had this man been *living* on the island? It was supposed to be deserted.

The man stirred, then got to his feet with a wince. She took a step back as he stretched to his full height. Geez, he was tall, with wide shoulders and muscular arms. His hair was long and tied at the nape.

"Dammit, that bloody hurts," he said.

She tilted her head at his accent. Was it Scottish? Here in Japan?

"Are you all right?" she asked warily. "Can I—"

"You need to leave the island," he interrupted.

"Hey, just wait a second." She crossed her arms. He might be ridiculously attractive, but he sure wasn't polite. "Who exactly are you?"

He took a step toward her, staggering on his injured leg. "My name is Aidan Hearst."

She narrowed her eyes at him. "How did you get here?"

"I live here."

"Yeah, right," she said. "In the middle of the Dragon Vortex?"

"Well, I'm here, aren't I? And this"—he pointed to Takeshi, who was sitting by his feet—"is my dog."

As the implications of that sunk in, she ran her tongue along her upper lip and jerked her head to move her hair out of her eyes.

"And you are?" he asked.

She cleared her throat, trying to ignore the heat that was rising in her cheeks. "I'm Rhianna Mori. And…well, I'm sorry. I guess I was given bad information. I was told the island was uninhabited."

He shrugged. "I don't advertise my presence."

"I guess not." With effort, she tore her gaze from him and looked around. "Did you see where that tiger went?"

He paused a beat before responding. "Not exactly."

She ran her hand through her tangled hair. She really

wished she'd seen the direction the tiger had gone. It would have helped her figure out which way to go to make her more permanent camp. *The opposite direction.*

Could the missing people have been eaten by the tiger? Perhaps there were more of them and they'd been here for years. Her thoughts whirled with scenarios, of the big cats attacking men as they slept. Eww.

She glanced at Aidan Hearst. What did he know of the disappearances? She would have to quiz him later. Right now, the only thing that concerned her was not running into that tiger again.

4

Dillon Savage snapped his head around to look at his director, Sean Holiday. "Did you see that?" A tiger had just stalked into the screen, and Rhianna had shot it before hurrying back toward the camera and turning it off. The Livestream video had gone black.

"Yeah. That was some awesome footage. Prime ratings stuff," Sean said, setting a schedule calendar aside. "And we didn't have to pay extra for it. I hope that beast hangs around. She needs to keep that damn camera on, though."

"Hey, she has a gun?" a cameraman asked. "I hope someone check to see if she knows how to use it," he snorted.

Dillon's jaw clenched. He rolled his eyes skyward. *If You Dare* had become all about the ratings. In another episode, a guy had gotten bitten by a cobra. And while it was great for ratings, he'd nearly died. Thank god they had a team of medics on board the yacht—ex-marine types who were pretty darn good, if unconventional. "You don't want me to go back there, do you?"

Sean blew a puff of cigar smoke out the corner of his mouth. "Don't worry your handsome head. We'll take protection when we return to get her."

"So you're just going to leave her out there...alone?"

"She'll be fine. And she signed a release." Sean got up and walked to the door. "I'm going topside to get some fresh air."

Dillon fisted his hands. If the money weren't so good, he would *not* be doing this show. "You're a heartless bastard," he muttered.

Sean raised an eyebrow at Dillon. "Remember that. And don't cross me.

She was heading the wrong direction—inland instead of out to the sandbar where she'd been dropped off.

Dammit.

Aidan paced in a tight circle and then paused to stare at Takeshi, who looked up at him with his big, dark eyes as if to say, *Well, aren't you going after her?*

He turned and followed her, grumbling to himself as he went. She couldn't make it easy and flee the island. No, she gathered her things and headed inland instead.

Aidan walked after her, not sure how he could force her to leave. He could hear her traversing the forest floor, with the snap of twigs beneath her slight weight, and her delicate cinnamon scent wafted to him on the breeze.

At the same time, the voice in his head was whispering how dangerous it was for her to be here. Every moment she remained increased the probability that she would never escape this island, never escape Theodora.

A dull, sinking sensation settled in his stomach at the futility of it all. His days were usually pretty much the same. He tinkered with his inventions and kept watch against evil shit trying to get to his tree. Aka the mysterious and demonic creatures of the Dark Realm.

The terrain dipped downward before it rose again, and Aidan continued to follow Rhianna. A chain of mountains circled the inner valley, and she took the course of least resistance along the base of the mountains. They were coming to the center, where the ground was soft and slick with moisture. Nearby, a stream flowed, washing over boulders and fallen tree limbs. As he walked, he began to notice the paths he'd worn through the forest. He hadn't realized he'd done that, but he supposed it made sense. It also made it easy for her to travel without resistance.

And led her straight to the most critical spots on the island...such as where he lived.

Rhianna came to a clearing where the sky opened up over a small pond of translucent blue-green water. The place was magnificent, a fairy-tale abode. At the far side of the pool there was a wide arched bridge of rock. It was cave-like, yet around twenty feet or so inside the space, it opened up again with an enormous hole in the ceiling, where the sky shown through. A waterfall spilled through the opening, creating a drumming rhythm as water gushed into the pool. The setting was architecturally brilliant in its interlocking curves and structure and texture. A miracle only Mother Nature could create.

"So beautiful," she whispered. Her eyes widened as she took it all in.

For several minutes, she stood there watching the water turn to white mist as it poured into the pool. It almost seemed magical. She inhaled the earthy fragrance, so different from the ocean on the coast.

She didn't want to move lest she break the enchantment

of this fantasy place, and she desperately wished the camera allowed for zooming in and out. But it didn't. She'd had to move to get a closer look. Finally, she cleared her throat, "This seems like one of those spectacular finds for *National Geographic*. My words won't do it justice, folks. But as you can see, this place is enchanting."

A strange resistance washed over her. Part of her didn't want to share this place with an audience, a selfish desire to keep the stunning locale to herself. But it wasn't exactly to herself, she realized. Aidan had probably been here. He could even be following her now.

She set the GoPro aside and breathed deeply, taking in the moist air, and then exhaled with abandon. A giggle bubbled up and echoed off the grotto. This was what freedom and secrecy and a mixture of recklessness and delight felt like. She was in her own world now.

Giving into the spell of the place, she glanced about, making sure she was alone. Then, stepping behind a plant with large tropical leaves, she stripped off her clothes. After another quick look around, she dropped into the water.

The ground immediately fell away. The pool was deep and warm, like a hot spring. It was heaven after spending the night on the damp, hard ground. The water felt more buoyant than any pool she'd ever experienced, too; it must have a very high salt content. She dove deep and kicked back to the surface. She floated on her back and gazed up through the trees overhead.

Soon, her attention turned to the waterfall. She wondered if there was a cave behind the falls. She'd heard of that. Curious, she swam beneath the stone arch. As she popped up on the other side, a shadow fell, blocking the sun. Her heart pounded in her chest. If something happened, she was completely on her own.

As she came closer to the waterfall, another space in the rocks opened above her. Water poured over a ledge into the pond, spraying over her head. It was ice-cold, a sharp contrast to the warm water of the depths. She gasped as she inched closer to the slapping white foam, peering through the flowing sheet of water.

Geez, that's cold.

She shivered and swam backward. Maybe she'd investigate the waterfall more later.

She rotated into a sidestroke and savored the rise in temperature as she traveled back to the warmer side of the pond. A long sigh escaped her lips as she looked around. Up on the rocks where she'd left her things, a movement caught her attention. She began to tread water and squinted to see into the shadows.

OMG. The tiger!

The effing tiger stood over her belongings. She tensed, sunk beneath the surface—hoping he wouldn't notice her—and came up again sputtering. With her heart thumping in her throat, she swam in reverse, putting more distance between them. God, she hoped tigers didn't like to swim.

As if the big cat understood her dilemma, he lumbered along the path to a large rock. He sat, looking back at her, seeming to give her space. But Rhianna didn't trust the animal. Her breathing quickened as she imagined the damage those huge claws could do. Could she retrieve her clothes and ease on out of here in one piece?

As if he were disinterested, the tiger turned and moved to the other side of pond.

Slowly, she floated toward the rocks. She climbed to the ledge, all the while keeping a watchful eye on the tiger. He was near enough to make out the black irises and golden-green rims of his eyes. He lowered his head, restrained, and turned away.

With controlled movements, she slid on her panties and bra, shirt, pants, and shoes. The tiger almost seemed as if he were asleep. *Almost.* She wouldn't have faith in that assumption, though. It was too risky.

Carefully she hefted her satchel and walked backward, toe to heel, to maintain her balance on the slippery rocks. The tiger lifted his head and cocked it to the side.

Nope, he wasn't sleeping.

The pounding in her rib cage increased. So close and yet... No, she would just keep on walking, slowly and calmly. She needed to find a shelter where the tiger wouldn't bother her. But was that even possible?

As if a humongous tree had fallen, a boom echoed through the forest, and the ground shook.

What was that? An earthquake?

Rhianna swept her gaze around the area. She didn't notice anything unusual...at first. Then her attention settled on the tiger again. As she watched, the cat morphed into a man, and her jaw dropped, letting in much-needed oxygen. The gorgeously tall, well-built specimen of manliness she had met earlier, seemed every bit in tune with the tiger he'd sprung from, but he wasn't gazing back at her. Instead, his expression was twisted with fury as he stared off to the side of the pool. Suddenly, a woman magically marched right out of a slab of rock.

Rhianna rubbed her eyes. What the hell was going on? She wanted to get the heck out of there, but her feet wouldn't budge. Her body trembled, curving in on itself in a protective stance. He...he had changed right before her eyes into Aidan Hearst. And then another stranger just appeared as if out of thin air? It wasn't possible. But if it was...

Oh god. Had he been watching her swim naked the entire time?

She flinched at the notion. However, given the situation, it seemed an absurd thing to worry about right now. She cast it out of her mind and refocused. Something way weirder was going down.

5

Aidan kept his eyes on Theodora as the mountain moved and shifted and she walked out of her world and into his.

Well, fuck. Rhianna's time was already up.

There was only one place she'd be safe—his Divine Tree. He burst into a run toward her. Her eyes grew wide as he approached her, and he reached out to grab her hand and tug her with him.

His strong fingers enveloped hers. "Come," he commanded.

She narrowed her gaze on him, and the next thing he knew her other arm had come up and shoved his arm out of the way. Then her leg swung around like a fan, struck him in the side of his head. He went down, flipping over in the process and landing flat on his back. She stood above him looking strong and mighty fine in a defensive karate stance, shooting daggers from her eyes at him.

Staring up at her, he was shocked by the precision move. As air returned to his lungs, he let out a painful gasp. He lifted his feet, rolling higher onto his shoulder blades, then snapped his legs downward while going airborne. With a jerk, he landed on his feet. "What the hell are you doing, woman? I'm trying to save you."

"You...you just transformed into a man from a *fucking tiger*. What are you?" she bit out.

"We'll get to that when you're safe." He tried to keep his voice even. But he wouldn't brook any argument, and he wouldn't give her a choice. He took her hand again and pulled her after him. It was either she moved her feet willingly or he'd carry her.

"My things," she said, dismissing his commanding demeanor and dragging her feet.

He kept going. "You don't need them."

"Yes, I do. I need my video equipment. This is exactly the sort of thing I was sent here to document," she said adamantly.

Just then, Theodora hurdled balls of energy at them that burst into flames just off to the side of where they stood. The heat of the blast scorched across his legs. Rhianna yelped, more out of shock than injury, given she didn't seem wounded. But still, Theodora's aggression infuriated him. She seemed angrier than usual. What had happened to instigate the change?

"Don't interfere, Aidan," Theodora growled.

They raced along a narrow path that circle the pond and cut into the space where two mountains met. At the back of the opening, a tunnel took them between the ridges, a tight hallway that led into another opening on the other side. In this valley, his Divine Tree stood proud and tall with its branches stretching wide and touching the ground.

When he came to the hidden opening and hurriedly acknowledged the tree, he entered, taking Rhianna along with him. Inside the great oak, he paused, breathing hard. This was the first time he'd brought someone inside the tree. And Custos had let them in. Good. Good. In retrospect, there had not been time to reflect on whether the tree would allow her entrance. His breath slowed. But he'd had little choice. It was imperative they escape Theodora.

Once they were safely inside the tree, he released her hand. She rubbed the blood back into it with her other hand. Then took in her surroundings. She slapped her palm against cheek and then ran it up over her forehead in awe. "Holy shit."

"I'm sorry I didn't have time to prepare you for this." He watched her reaction. This was normal to him, but he supposed it would be shocking to the average human.

"Prepare me? I don't think that's possible," she said in awe.

He allowed her a minute to take in the sanctuary of the tree. He hadn't stopped to admire its beauty in a long time, and he tried to see it as she would. The endless paths of smooth golden wood glowed. The way it seemed so much bigger from within. The magical quality it elicited. He watched her face as she took it all in. Somehow he thought she saw with more than just her eyes…he sensed an extra ability, perhaps. He couldn't allow her to stay in here. The tree and its secrets were sacred, after all.

"Let's go," he said. "She can't get you in here."

"Who is *she*?" She gave him a piercing glare.

"I'll get to that." He led the way down to a hallway that led to his quarters, allowing the pup to follow at will. He explained as they walked. "Theodora is a siren of sorts. She's a misplaced Valkyrie warrior with magical powers. She rules over an alternative universe and captures people and traps them within it. As far as I know, she possesses the only means of entering that world. To get in, she must take them over or let them in. And if they go, they don't come back."

She halted, shaking her head. "Wait a minute. What are

you talking about? What alternate universe? That's the stuff of science fiction," she said in disbelief.

"I assure you, there are many strange things in this world you don't know about," he said.

She grew quiet, seeming to think it through. "I came to the Dragon Vortex on a quest: to figure out what had happened to all those people who never returned after coming here. Maybe this alternate universe has something to do with that," she said, despite the skepticism on her face.

"People stay away from here for a reason, honey. You should have, too." His voice had a sarcastic bite to it.

She bristled at his use of 'honey.' As if to herself, she said, "I wish someone had told my great-grandfather that."

"What?"

Her dark-brown eyes locked on him. "He was from Sendai, Japan, actually closer to Nabekura Castle. My research indicates, he came to this island around 1922, and then no one heard from him again. My grandfather came to the States sometime after that and married. Go a little further down the line, and here I am."

He nodded ever so slightly and considered his lack of ancestry for a moment. Since he was immortal, his line went very far back in time. Yet the mind still plays weird tricks sometimes and makes it seem like yesterday.

Inside his home, after navigating a few hallways and turns, they came to the main living area and the kitchen. The bar was over to the right against the wall. She marched over to it, popped the stopper on a bottle of his best Scotch, and poured herself a glass.

"Okay," she said. "Start from the beginning. Tell me the story of Dragon Vortex." She angled the glass to her lips and took a sip.

He couldn't blame her. He supposed what she'd just witnessed would shake anyone out of their boots. She'd earned a drink.

Her eyes met his over the rim of her glass, held, and

then she tipped back her head and downed the rest of the liquor.

Only the moisture in her eyes, gave a hint that the drink burned on the way down. He poured a glass and followed her lead.

Then she collapsed into a nearby club chair of tufted glove leather. She gazed at him from beneath long, lush eyelashes. The look in her eyes was raw, confused, and weary. His gut twisted. No matter what, her world would never be the same again.

Her head spun at the unbelievable shit that was happening. The tiger had transformed into a man before her eyes, and an odd creature—she didn't want to call her a *woman* because she seemed incongruously beyond mere mortal— had materialized out of nowhere.

She thought of her Pilate class and friends at home with longing. She remembered Terri's hug and admonishment to be careful and have fun. Rhianna gave a sad laugh. This was neither.

Aidan—if that was truly his name—poured her another shot of whiskey. The thought that she should be drinking sake instead played through her befuddled mind. Even so, she drank a swig of the amber liquid in her glass. Not the whole thing this time, but enough to savor the warmth of it trickling down.

He chuckled, causing her to lift her head to look at him. "I thought women preferred wine or mint juleps or something," he said.

She shrugged. "Not this one."

"So I see."

"Okay..." She blew out a deep breath. "What kind of rabbit hole have I fallen down?"

He frowned.

"You know, *Alice In Wonderland?* She chased a rabbit down— Oh never mind." She shook her head, then took another sip and sighed. He had a definite Scottish accent, so maybe he would familiar with classic books. But he did live far from civilization on an island. Had he always lived here?

"I try to keep up with the rest of the world, but—"

"Never mind." She waved a dismissive hand as the alcohol began to loosen the tight rein she held on her emotions.

He dipped his chin to his chest.

Had she somehow hurt his feelings? A tightness twisted beneath her breastbone at that, but why did it even concern her? She was the one in this bizarre situation.

When he looked up, air rushed out of her lungs. His gaze did something to her. Those hazel eyes with those thick lashes made her want to listen to him, believe him. Even through her anger and anxiety, a warmth nudged her tummy. She tried to shoo the sensation away.

Finally, he spoke. "Prepare yourself," he warned her. "You've stumbled upon something no one knows exists. The tree we entered is called a Divine Tree, or tree of life. I am its immortal Guardian."

She barked out a laugh without meaning to. It didn't matter how handsome he was, this was absolutely ridiculous. "Immortal? Like you don't die? And you guard the tree of life?"

"Oh, I can die. But only under certain circumstances. Otherwise, no."

She tried to absorb the information, tried not to dismiss it instantly again, but she shook her head. "And you're telling me you can somehow shift into a tiger, too?"

He nodded. "And an eagle."

She straightened. He was a double shape-shifter? She squinted at him. "How old are you?" she asked, not totally prepared to hear the answer.

"My body doesn't age like yours, so it doesn't really matter. But... I was born in 1094 AD."

"You've got to be kidding me." She opened her mouth, then closed it. She fought a gasp, trying to pretend she could handle it. "That's a helluva long time ago."

"Yes, it is." He leaned an elbow against the bar. "Except age is irrelevant to me. I'm essentially the same as I was when I was charged with the duty of Guardian."

Everything about this situation was hard to believe. From being on the island to listening to his rich voice with a hint of a Scottish accent—she needed to learn more about that—to these incredible tales he was spinning. It couldn't actually be true.

Could it?

But with what she'd witnessed with her own eyes, something inside her knew what he said was somehow possible. Even though she couldn't comprehend how it could be, and as much as she wanted to deny it, she *was* in the presence of an immortal shape-shifter.

Unable to sit any longer, she rose and moved randomly about. On the wall above the bar hung a clock comprised of large metal gears. It looked custom designed with its intricate overlaid metal pieces, and she wondered if he had made it. She admired the work and glanced around, wondering how he had gotten all these magnificent decorations to this remote island.

Then she shook herself as the magnitude of everything she didn't know slammed into her. She moved back to the chair, ready to hear all the wretched details. "All right, give it to me. Tell me the whole story."

He stared at her, his jaw set firm, his tone dry. "I was sent here as a Guardian of the Divine Tree. There are many beings out there that will do anything to get their hands on the secrets of the universe, which the tree holds, and it's my job to see that doesn't happen."

"Wow. That's a weighty responsibility." She smiled, but then it abruptly faded.

He nodded once. "Very."

"And the…the woman chasing us?"

"Theodora. She rules over Riam, an alternate universe to ours. She won't just let you go."

Rhia furrowed her brow. "But why would she even want me?"

"Think of her as a ruler in the Ancient Roman Empire. She kidnaps people to be her subjects, her gladiators of sorts. And the more people she rules, the more entertainment she gets. Plus somehow her power grows." He held Rhianna's gaze, his voice warming. "And you're clearly a fighter. She will most definitely be interested in you."

6

To say that Theodora was a bad sport was an understatement. She stood on the highest peak on the southernmost tip of the island looking out to sea. That Guardian asshole wouldn't give her the female. Aidan Hearst actually *hid* her. He'd never cared what she'd done with her captives before!

However, it didn't matter. He had no control over what she did. Period.

Theodora made a tsking sound. *They cannot stay underground forever.*

For now, at least there was a ship about five miles from the shore. The people's voices had drifted to her last night while they were drinking and carousing. It would make a nice diversion.

She disappeared, riding on air until she was close to the yacht. There were three men aboard—two up top, one down below. From where she stood, she used her magic to untie the ropes that held the dinghy in place and set it free.

There would be no escaping by that little boat. Not that she wouldn't get them, regardless. It quickly drifted away.

The men were drinking coffee. She recognized the pleasant aroma. Extending her scepter toward the men, she wrapped them like a package in a clear net. They didn't know what hit them. She smiled. *Giftwrapped for the games.*

"You like games, don't you?" she asked.

The men stared at her, their eyes huge, confused, disbelieving, and full of fear. They pushed against the bonds, climbing over one another trying to escape. The slender, handsome man scrambled on top of the bald man's head and face, giving him a bloody nose.

Theodora smiled. With a steady hand on her sorcerer's staff, she opened a porthole to Riam. The blue orb at the head of the staff glowed, showering energy in front of her. She floated the men up through it.

She sighed. She'd grown bored of late with her fighting games. Perhaps it was time to add a new element. But what would up the excitement? She tapped a finger against her chin.

Spectators!

Oh yes. That was it. She would send out some invitations to those she knew in the Dark Realm. It had been a long time since she'd had any company.

A lengthy silence filled the kitchen as Aidan realized he had a guest for the first time in hundreds of years. Archangel Seth and his *delegato* were the only people who had been in his home.

"Would you like something to eat?" he finally asked.

Her eyes lit up. "Yes, please. That would be nice."

He smiled while internally kicking himself. *Of course she'd want to eat.*

Minutes later, he was in the kitchen digging through the

refrigerator to find something he could make. He
scrambled a few eggs to serve with some smoked fish and
a portion of rice.

"Thank you," she said with sincere appreciation.

"You're welcome."

He looked at her briefly. She lounged at a small table,
watching him cook. Her chin rested on the heel of her
hand as she leaned over the table. She looked tired. But
what had she expected coming to a deserted island?

He scolded himself. She'd been through a lot today. He
needed to cut her some slack. "This will be much better
than what you had for breakfast."

She squinted at him. "How would you...?" Her eyes
grew rounder, wider, as recognition sparked. "It was you...
The tiger watching me swim in the pond."

He tried to hide the wicked smile that tugged at his lips
but failed miserably. "It was the best entertainment I've
had in centuries."

"Well, this is the only time I'll probably ever hear that
line." Her mouth pulled up at one corner into a cute
lopsided smile.

He raised a brow. "Line?"

She shook her head and glanced down. "It doesn't
matter." After a beat, she lifted her chin and met his eyes.
"Look, tiger or not, you should have walked away and
given me privacy. If you were a gentleman, you would
have."

"In case you haven't noticed, we're in the middle of a
wooded forest, six hundred miles from civilization. There
are no gentlemen anywhere near here."

She laughed. It felt like rain falling after a severe
draught. He longed to reach across and touch her hand.
Just to see how soft her skin was. Just to feel her pulse
beat beneath his fingertips. Just to confirm she was a real,
live woman here in his quarters.

While she ate, he noted everything about her—her

scent drifting over to him, the way her fork clinked and scraped over the plate, her hair brushing her cheek when she tipped her head forward to take another bite.

He gave a controlled inhale and exhale. Gritting his teeth, he stood and stepped away, taking the now-empty dishes with him. As he cleaned up, he resisted looking back at her and taking in her loveliness.

Alone. Alone. Alone. He reminded himself that was the kind of life he was meant to lead. But for the first time ever—maybe because two of his brothers had recently found their mates—he wondered, just for a moment, that perhaps he might have that same kind of companionship someday.

Swallowing, he shrugged off the foolish thoughts. He couldn't condemn anyone to the life of solitude that was his existence. But regardless, he wanted to keep her from the clutches of Theodora even more than he had before.

A puppy's bark brought him out of his thoughts. "Takeshi," he said. He glanced at Rhianna apologetically. "I forgot about the pup."

Quickly, he set about rectifying the situation. He headed down the hall, out of sight, and opened the door where he heard the dog. Takeshi sprung out the door immediately vaulting to their visitor.

She allowed the pup to leap into her lap where he licked her face. A soft laugh bubbled from her as she petted the animal.

"Takeshi, off," Aidan commanded. When he didn't obey, Aidan went over, removed the pup from her lap, and set him on the floor, repeating the instruction. "I'm sorry. I've only had him a few days so he has yet to learn."

Her smile practically reached her ears this time. "Of course. He's just a puppy." She leaned forward and stroked the dog's head. "Takeshi. I like that name."

For a second, he thought he glimpsed her genuine personality, free from the worries of her current dilemma.

"It means *warrior*," he explained.

"I like it."

He felt lightness inside his chest, a pleasant hum. "Since I live alone, my dogs aren't exactly trained to live with people."

"You have other animals?"

"Only this one right now."

She scratched Takeshi's head. "Well, he's adorable."

Aidan didn't say anything, simply watched her interact with the dog. She was enchanting. Could this be the same female who had landed him on his back a short time ago?

With a mental shake of his head, he stood. He had her safe inside his home now.

So what was he going to do next?

7

"Would you like a tour of the place? Aidan asked Rhianna.

She looked into Aidan's hazel eyes, which held deep green and gold tones. *Tiger eyes.* "Yes. That would be nice."

Plus, she might discover the ins and outs of the place for when she left. While he may have come to her aid in regards to the sorceress, Rhia had no delusions that she wouldn't eventually have to find her way back to camp and contact the TV crew.

Takeshi jumped up and put himself in front of Aidan. She laughed. "Looks like someone would like to come along."

Aidan moved his hand forward, signaling the dog to come along. "This is the living area," he started. "As you can see, it's kind of just one big room but there are separate designated spots for the kitchen, living room, and bar."

She nodded, then looked up the center of the space to

a stained glass skylight window far above them. The hues of red, gold, green, and blue reflected off the walls. "What's up there?"

"A library. It's the only room that's situated aboveground and has a window."

With a sweeping glance, she noticed a fairly new TV and a stack of movies sitting on a table. It occurred to her then that lights were on. "You have electricity?"

"Yes," he said. "It's generated on the island and stored in large battery cells."

"Interesting. How does it work?"

He smiled. "I'll show you when we get to that area. Since I live here alone, I do everything myself. I have nothing but time, and I love to tinker with things."

They kept walking. "The sleeping and bathing quarters are down that hall." He pointed to the right but continued forward.

Next they came to a large area where the floor was cut away, revealing a lower level. She peered over the railing. A circular staircase wound down to the next floor. The space around the stairs was filled with stuff sitting on tables, and chairs, and on the floor. An easel with paints and brushes was set up, and there was a workbench with pieces of metal, nuts, bolts, and other tools, including a ban saw and table.

"My goodness. How did you get all that in here?" she asked. "And…well, where did it all come from?"

"You'd be surprised what washes ashore. Some of it came from abandoned ships, too, and other things came from Amazon."

She jerked her head around to stare at him. "Really?" Given where and how he lived, she had assumed he didn't have modern access to things, especially the Internet. It was a quite naive guess on her part. "Can I go down there?"

He held out his palm. "Be my guest."

Together they tromped to the bottom of the deep room. She looked around, taking everything in. "The room looks as if it's carved out of the stone."

"You're very observant. That's exactly how it was formed. A little at a time, over several centuries. As my collection grew, so did the room."

She walked around, noting the antiques intermingled with present-day items, including several examples of assembly line machines on timers. Her jaw dropped, and then she snapped her mouth closed. She'd never seen anything like it in her entire life.

"Wow, this is…just wow!" she said. "How did you learn how to make all this?"

He shrugged. "I read a lot of books."

"I can't wait to see your library, then," she said on a laugh.

They leaned toward each other, and their eyes met. A warmth swept over her, and she looked away, a thought occurring to her. "Has anyone ever seen this before?"

"No."

The straightforward answer made her nervous—he wasn't used to being with people. Wild…the word flitted through her head. Like the wild dog she'd first thought Takeshi was. She eased as nonchalantly as she could to the other end of a counter filled with metal parts. Here she was, alone with a *shape-shifter*. She couldn't believe she was even using that word. Why wasn't she huddled in a corner shaking in her shoes?

Because he'd been nothing but kind to her. And his voice was quiet and soothing and sexy.

She blinked at that last part.

"Come this way and I'll show you where the electricity is generated," he suggested.

She nodded and followed him down some damp stairs and into another large, open area. She studied the room. "This one is only partially man-made," she noted aloud.

"On the other side it looks like a natural cave."

"Very good." He smiled. "This is located near the waterfall, where another hole in the earth allows water to flow into a subterranean pool. I use a microhydro power to generate power."

"Hydro? So you use water to make electricity?"

He leaned his massive shoulder against the wall. "Exactly. And I also pump the water to the kitchen and bath."

"It looks like you have the perfect setup here."

"If you have to live on an island in the middle of the ocean, you can't get much better than this." He flashed her another smile.

"I think you're right about that."

They turned together, and he waited for her lead the way back to the living area, or so she presumed. As they went, she noticed the echo of their footsteps off the walls this time. She retraced her steps to the staircase and ascended to the living floor.

As she returned to where they had started, she made a mental note of everything. There were probably a lot of things that would surprise her in the world and what she'd encountered today would surely rank among them. And as kind as Aidan seemed, she may only have one chance to get out of here and make her way home.

"So…" She turned to him. "Now what?"

He shrugged. "You should stay here tonight. Tomorrow I'll get your things so you can contact your people to pick you up."

She nodded. She hated giving up on the whole *If You Dare* thing, but given the circumstances, she didn't see an alternative any longer. As unbelievable as this whole day had seemed, she could feel deep in her gut that Aidan wasn't lying to her about Theodora and her kidnappings. She was dangerous and obviously running the show.

Rhianna swallowed, hard. She had come here to figure

out why her great grandfather had disappeared. Now she had a pretty good idea.

"Where will I sleep?" she asked. "I'd like to freshen up."

Aidan twisted to peer at her. "You can have my room," he said over his shoulder. Since he never had guests, he'd had no need for a guest room. His was the only bedroom. He could easily sleep on the couch.

"Are you sure? I don't want to put you out." She licked her lips nervously.

He looked at her and felt completely out of his element, even though he was in his own home.

A series of tapes, movies, and videos skated through his head as he searched for the right response. Well, she *was* putting him out. But he hadn't had much practice in dealing with people. Sure, he spoke to his brothers, four times a year he traveled to the mainland, and he had a few ham radio and computer friends. The satellite communication system he'd bought had been worth every penny. He occasionally chatted with an old angel named Seth, as well, and every once in a great while he fought a demon or two, but that was the extent of his experience with communication.

"I'm tough. I can handle the sofa," he said with a wink. It was beyond true. Back in the beginning when he'd first come to the island, he'd slept on the ground and used whatever he could find on the island to make himself as comfortable as possible. "Don't worry about me."

Her brow furrowed, and she nodded slowly.

He could handle just about anything. But the thought of a female in his bed…? That was a different matter.

8

When Aidan heard water running in the bath, he wondered if he should retrieve Rhianna's things now instead of in the morning, if for no other reason than so she could have a fresh change of clothes. The sun had already set as his eagle flew out of the opening near the waterfall and soared over the island. It felt good to expend the energy that had been coiled inside him all day. He executed a wide circle around the area, surveying it for any sign of Theodora. He saw none.

As he landed near Rhianna's satchel, he changed seamlessly into his human form. Still no sorceress, but that didn't mean she'd left. He grabbed the bag and slung it over one shoulder. It only weighed about twenty pounds or so, he guessed, and he wondered what she'd brought with her. His mind conjured up the image of lacy underthings like the ones he'd seen in movies, and the thought of her in them awakened a sleeping giant within him.

He growled. He was still a man, after all, even though

he'd worked mighty hard to deny that part of him. Trying to scrub the thoughts from his mind, he lumbered through the grotto passageway between the mountains toward home. As he leaped down to the ground from a huge rock, the Divine Tree signaled him through the tattoos on his back and wrist, which were now suddenly burning. He immediately burst into a run. The tree only reached out like that when there was danger nearby.

Something was up. When he came upon the tree, he halted. Theodora was lounging beneath it. She extended her scepter overhead and stabbed at the tree's branches. "I thought you'd come running," the sorceress murmured.

He glared at her. "Why don't you go back to your world, *Theo*?"

She shot to her feet. "You're itching for a fight, are you? Just call me that again."

"Seems we're going to tangle no matter what I say," he said with a sneer.

"Just hand over the female and I'll be on my way."

He scoffed. "Not going to happen."

"Ah, sweetie, don't be like that." A burst of energy pulsed from the ornate orb on the top of her scepter. "I need more females. This one is mine."

He watched the magic flying toward him and lifted his foot in the air. The powerful ball of fire landed precisely where his boot had been.

The Divine Tree whirled its branches, hitting Theodora in the shoulder. She sidestepped, laughter bubbling from her lips. "Is that all you have? Really?"

Do not get drawn in by her, Custos warned.

It's a game she plays, he replied.

Not this time. There's something more.

"What? Not including me in the conversation?" Theodora asked. "Not nice. Not nice at all." She shot another ball of energy into a stand of pines and splintered them into firewood.

"Go home," he demanded through clenched teeth. "The girl is *mine* to do with as I choose." Even he was surprised at the word—he hadn't planned on saying that—but possession was a sentiment Theodora understood. He was also shocked at the feelings of protectiveness of and connection to Rhianna that stirred within him.

"No, Guardian. I don't play that way. Hide her if you will, but if I catch her, she will become a ward of my kingdom. And she will *not* enjoy it."

With that, the sorceress disappeared.

Despite the threat, the tension in Aidan's muscles eased. He slung the satchel over his shoulder again and walked through a secret entrance into his home.

He hated that Rhianna was stuck in the middle of the feud that was brewing between good and evil. Perhaps it was time to call his brothers and apprise them of what was going on here. Only one side would win. And although he didn't doubt it would be his side, he also understood there would be many casualties before the battle was over. He couldn't let Rhianna be one of them.

9

Rhianna was in the kitchen fixing herself a cup of coffee when he entered. She glanced over her shoulder at him, saw the satchel, and turning, balancing on one foot, threw her arms around him. "Oh, you wonderful man!"

Every nerve in his body responded to her touch as a spark zinged through him. She lowered her eyelids and looked into his eyes, making him believe she felt it, too. He slid a hand to the middle of her back and held her steady.

"I figured you may need something inside." Closing his eyes, he inhaled her scent, realizing the soap from his bathroom smelled different on her than it did on him. He took a second whiff, reluctant to let her go as she ended the embrace and took a step back.

She swallowed nervously as she lifted the cup she was working on when he'd entered.

From beneath his lashes, he watched her take a sip of her coffee. He gently tossed the bag on the table.

"Easy," she said.

He raised an eyebrow. "If it breaks after that, then it's not worth anything."

"It has my equipment inside. Well, it's not really *mine*, but still." She turned to put her back against the counter and held the cup with both hands.

"What's it for?"

"I'm here as part of a reality show. I was supposed to live alone on the island for three weeks and document my experience. We were hoping to discover why so many people have disappeared in Dragon Vortex. And if I make it the entire time, then I win a cash prize."

"A reality show?"

"Yes. They film it live and then put it on TV later."

He nodded. "Well, then I'm not sorry you failed. I don't want my island on television."

She straightened her spine. "I haven't failed yet."

"What are you talking about? We're getting you off this island as soon as possible. You have your belongings. You can contact your people tomorrow."

"But I've been thinking... What if I just hang around here until my three weeks are up? Get enough footage to make the director happy, and then they get their show and I get to learn more..." Her lips pressed together.

He narrowed his eyes. She seemed to be keeping something from him... he sensed there was another reason. "You're hiding something. What?"

She shrugged. "Nothing."

"Tell me."

"I'm here to discover more about my heritage. My great-grandfather disappeared somewhere around here. I was hoping to figure out what happened to him."

"That was a long time ago, correct?"

"Yes," she said dejectedly. "Maybe he was lost in a ship crossing. Or eaten by a tiger."

"Humph. I'm the only tiger in these parts. And I assure you, I didn't eat him."

"But...you wouldn't have been around then, right."

He dipped his chin and glanced at her past his hooded brows.

"Wait. I understand. You were alive back then. Wow."

"And what do I get if you stay?" He approached her, staring at her mouth, then eyes.

She looked at him long and hard, as if measuring what she was going to say before she spoke. He could hear her pulse kick up to a rapid pace, revealing her lack of confidence.

"You will get a companion for a three weeks." She gave him a beguiling smile.

Her words were a punch in his gut that he hadn't seen coming, and desire flooded every part of his being. His brows shot towards his hairline. He stepped closer and put his hands on her shoulders, drawing her near.

"A no-frills c-companion," she stammered, scooting backward. When there was a bit of distance between them, she crossed her arms over her chest.

He caught her reluctance and, with a slow smile, matched her stance. "You've known me all of...six hours and this is your plan?"

She shrugged and shifted her weight.

He had to admit her proposal was damned tempting. No one had been on the island for that length of time. Not even the crazy archangel, Seth, stayed for long.

Three weeks.

He filled his lungs with air and held the breath until his heart hammered against his ribs, then released it with a controlled exhale.

"Before being so quick to stay here, let me share with you that I ran into Theodora again while I was getting your satchel. She seems quite intent on claiming you."

"And if I don't want to go to this universe of hers?" she countered.

"Like I told you before, it's not exactly an invitation. More like an abduction."

"Don't you have any authority over this island?" She gave a circular wave of a hand. "Can't you stop her with your shape-shifting powers and all?"

"I don't think so. I... I don't know. I've never tried. My duty has always lain elsewhere."

Her gaze narrowed on him. "Do you mean you've simply allowed her to take the others?"

"It was none of my affair."

"And now?" She stepped right up to him, chest to chest, challenging.

In one swift movement, he cupped a hand behind her head and drew her to him until his mouth firmly took hers in a searing kiss. To his delight, she kissed him back, opening her lips and meeting his tongue as he tasted her.

Abruptly, he came to his senses and released her. She fell back a few steps, catching herself against the counter.

"I don't want to see you get hurt or taken. You should leave first thing tomorrow." He spun on his heel and headed up the spiral staircase to the library. It had the only other bathroom in the place, plus a sofa to crash on. Not that he'd be able to sleep.

Rhianna touched her fingers to her lips, trying to hold back a smile. That had been extraordinary. She couldn't believe the way her body responded to Aidan's touch, his kiss. She'd gone all mushy inside.

She stood rooted in place and listened to the click of his steps until their tone changed. He must have reached the landing. Finally, she stepped back on rubbery legs. Geez, it was warm in here. She fanned her face.

As she ambled to the bedroom, she admitted he was right and she probably should call it quits. She hadn't been totally honest about her reason for staying. It wasn't the money. In truth, she came on the show to get answers.

She'd gotten some of those—to an extent. If she wanted to learn more, she had to stay.

An image of her grandfather dying without her invaded her thoughts. Was it worth not being with him? She might as well go home and spend the little time she had left with him. But something inside was begging her to stay.

She dropped, exhausted, on top of the covers, and his scent enveloped her. It was his bed after all.

From upstairs she heard a piano playing. Intrigued, and even though she was tired, she rose and followed the music. At the top rung of the stairs, she paused, trying to view past a bookcase into the room. She moved as quietly as she could. It reminded her of when she was a child and she used to hide behind the recliner in the living room to eavesdrop on her parents. She didn't want to be caught sneaking around by Aidan, but she was so curious.

"You can come in," he said without pausing in his playing. "I know you're there."

"I don't mean to interrupt. I just heard the music. It's beautiful." She walked over to the nearest chair, sat, and folded her feet beneath her bottom.

She looked around, immediately falling in love with the room. It was lined with tall, overflowing bookshelves, and in the center of the room was a grouping of furniture—a sofa, one chair, a coffee table, and an end table. Like downstairs, it seemed built for personal use as opposed to entertaining.

In the corner, Aidan was playing a grand piano. Her presence didn't seem to bother him, those large hands mastering the keys perfectly, his body swaying with the intensity of the piece. A longing stirred in her belly. Music did that to her. Hell, *he* did that to her, the voice in her head admitted.

When he finished, her heart was pounding. She clapped.

He angled his large frame sideways on the piano bench

and stared at her. Slowly, he lifted a whiskey glass from the top of the piano and drank.

Rhianna stood and strolled over to him. She stopped short of touching the piano, even though she wanted to. "I'm amazed. You're very good. How did you get a piano here?"

"Where there's a will there's a way," he recited. "Ships can carry anything. But getting it *in here* was another matter. I had to partly disassemble it"—he ran a hand lovingly over the wood—"and put it back together."

"Given what I've seen of your workroom, I guess that was a piece of cake for you."

He angled his head, obviously confused by the saying. For someone who read so many books, he was sure missing some modern idioms from his vocabulary.

"I mean that it was easy for you," she explained.

"I wouldn't say it was *easy*, but doable."

Her gaze slid past him, noting a violin and guitar sitting on stands. "Do you play those also?"

He shrugged. "I have a lot of time on my hands."

"Will you play something else, please?" She gave him an encouraging smile.

He nodded, placing his fingers on the keys.

Thirty minutes later, she was wondering again if packing up and leaving as he'd suggested was the best idea. Her heart yearned to spend just a little more time with him. Perhaps stay on the mainland and visit for a while. That would give her more time to investigate about her great-grandfather.

She shook her head at the way she was justifying her reasoning.

No, no. She was thinking like a lovesick teen.

"Thank you for letting me listen. I enjoyed it," she said, hoping he couldn't see her flushed face as she stood to go back downstairs.

She closed her eyes tightly and groaned inwardly. How

could she be attracted to a loner shape-shifter who lives in Japan? Nothing could ever come of it.

But it would be one hell of an adventure. One hell of thrill. One hell of a memory.

"Anytime," he replied. "Sleep well."

She nodded. "Good night, Aidan."

As she descended the stairs, she wondered why she always fell for the wrong men. Then she corrected herself. He wasn't just a man, was he?

10

When Rhianna awoke the next morning, she'd seen enough of golden eyes throughout the night in her dreams to predict that staying on the island wouldn't work. She knew it was just her brains working while she slept, but it felt like more. Could he have some special power over her? She shivered. Or was it her imagination working overtime? Even her curiosity couldn't sustain her for an entire three-quarters of a month under his watchful stare. Really, she must have been delusional last night when she'd proposed the idea.

Aidan was sitting in the living room when she entered. "Do you want to eat something before we leave?" he asked.

"No. Just coffee," she mumbled. She rolled her sleepy eyes. Evidently he was the chipper sort in the morning.

She plopped into a chair, and he delivered a piping hot cup to her. She took a sip. It was just right. "How did you know how I take my coffee?"

"I watched you last night. Plus, my keen sense of smell helps."

She angled her head, lifting a brow. "Is that because of your tiger?"

"Yes. Good guess."

She chewed on her fingernail for a moment. "It's still hard to believe...shape-shifting, I mean."

He nodded. "I imagine it seems impossible... Now how can you contact your team?"

His focus on getting her out of there stung, but she tried to ignore it. "I have satellite phone. The director and some other members of the crew are stationed on a ship not far away."

"After you finish your coffee, we'll go topside and call."

With a nod of agreement, she closed her eyes and drank. The warmth touching her mouth reminded her of his kiss last night. When she opened her eyes again, the same eyes that had haunted her sleep were watching her. She finished the last of her coffee in one more gulp and stood. "I'm ready," she announced.

A sadness pressed on her heart as she collected her satchel and met him at the entrance. They didn't speak as he led the way. She noted as they went the beauty of his home and everything he'd accomplished. She admired him for that. Which made her departure weigh heavier on her.

The next thing she knew, they were aboveground near the great tree. She still didn't know the whole story about the tree. "You know," she said, "if you chat on the ham radio or the Internet, perhaps we can keep in touch." Then one day he'd share everything with her, she thought.

"Uh, sure," he said.

But his response was without conviction. And it certainly wasn't filled with any of the passion she'd felt in his kiss. There she was again, back to that inescapable moment. She wondered now if she'd merely imagined the exchange or perhaps attributed more significance to the act than he'd intended. She decided it must be the latter.

Aidan stopped in a clearing up ahead. "You should have better reception here without the trees for interference."

She dug in her bag, pulled out the sat phone, powered it up, and dialed. She paced while it rang. He stood off to one side, waiting. No one picked up, so she ended the call and tried again. "Nope. I'm not sure it's going through."

"Let me see." He accepted the phone that she handed him and stared at its screen, reading the information there. "The signal strength seems okay. Sometimes the satellites go down, though, and an entire area is taken out."

"I don't know much about them," she admitted. But given his remote location, she guessed that's what he used on a regular basis.

He moved farther away from her and climbed a rocky bank, pointing the phone's antenna toward the sky. "I'm going to text them. Sometimes that gets through when a call doesn't."

"Okay." Rhianna hugged her arms around her middle. She watched as he manipulated the device, and she thought of all the gadgets and machines he had in his workshop.

Without warning, something lifted her feet off the ground and floated her forward. A scream ripped from her throat and the unnatural sensation made her feel as if she as enveloped in something, inside some kind of bubble. She turned her head to search out Aidan, but his attention was still on the phone.

"Help!" she yelled.

"It's too late," an icy voice sounded from within a haze.

Rhianna snapped her head around to find the sorceress, dressed in black, fitted garb with a flowing midnight-blue robe layered on top. An ornate warrior's breastplate showed beneath as well as a decoration of some kind of spiked armor over her left shoulder. In her right hand, she extended a scepter that was emitting a florescent blue-green glow. *Her power source*, Rhia guessed.

They were both moving into a swirl of blackness. Rhianna tried to tug free, straining in the opposite direction.

It was as if rock and dirt and trees created a funnel and she was about to be sucked into the whirlpool.

Again, Rhianna screamed for help. She looked toward Aidan. Finally, she appealed to him with her mind instead of her voice.

His eyes lifted and widened. His lips curled into an agonizing grimace, and he called her name. His feet raced forward as he tried to close the distance. His fist cut through the air, and then he transformed into a tiger and ate up the distance.

It was a futile effort, though. Both Theodora and Rhianna were traveling too quickly to be stopped. They passed into the darkness and the swirl of earthly hues closed in, smaller and smaller behind them.

The roar of a great cat shook her, even inside the bubble.

She was thrown from side to side like a marble being shaken within a cup. And then she was tossed unto the solid, dusty ground, landing hard and rolling to her knees. She glanced backward and up.

A porthole whirled shut.

The last thing Rhianna saw was the horror reflected in a pair of tiger's eyes.

In shock, she sat on the ground staring up at Theodora. That old saying from *The Wizard of Oz* echoed in her head: we're not in Kansas anymore. Her eyes darted around. Everything was a colorless gray with a heavy dose of barren and stark.

"That's right, sweetheart. Get a good look at your new home," Theodora said, seeming totally pleased with herself.

Rhianna stood. Instinctively she knew that it wasn't a good idea to aggravate her abductor, but she couldn't help saying, "You've made a mistake. I need to go back." She heard the panic rise in her own voice.

Theodora laughed. "They all say that."

Rhianna wondered how many people "they" were. She swallowed hard. The place smelled like dust, stale and old. Abruptly, like a cat who wasn't finished playing with a new toy, Theodora swished her scepter, floating Rhianna over the ground. She moved like a tumbleweed as Theodora flicked her around. When she finally released her, Rhianna was so disoriented she staggered, then halted, then staggered some more.

As the dizziness subsided, she noticed people entering the streets. Maybe this was just a ghost town movie set or something. It seemed that way. Maybe this was all a hoax. Maybe she was losing her mind.

She inhaled deeply and coughed on the stale air.

"Rhianna!"

She heard her name and turned. Dillon Savage ran into the street, Steve and Sean right behind him.

Oh god. The only people who knew exactly where she was were in this hellhole with her? She grabbed her stomach. Her lunch was threatening to spill.

"Now," Theodora remarked, "go join the other new recruits. The next war game is at five, so you'd best prepare."

Rhianna was about to ask what a war game was, but the sorceress vanished in a puff of smoke. Stunned, Rhia moved toward Savage and the men. She glanced along the street as she walked. Dozens and dozens of people were staring at her with empty eyes and sad faces.

Savage tugged her into the closest building. It was sparsely furnished inside—just an old sofa and some chairs. Again, she thought of a movie set. She'd watched programs on filming; she'd even considered film as a profession in her youth.

Rhianna wrapped her arms around her middle. None of this seemed real. It couldn't be real.

Aidan's roar did nothing to stop it. Theodora had been silent in her attack. He'd had no warning, no way to catch them, no way to leap through to the other side.

Without hesitation, he turned and sprinted toward the Divine Tree. He had only one chance to bring her back. That was, if Custos would give him the key to crossing.

He would go to the catacombs and appeal to the Divine Tree. He would even call upon Seth to guard the tree in Aidan's absence.

Changing into his human form, Aidan halted outside a space between the rocks. There, he slid into a hidden entrance that led to an underground passageway. "Seth! Seth!" He glanced up to the heavens, as if that would help summon the archangel. "Get your ass down here."

He didn't actually know if Seth was in heaven or hanging someplace else right now. He only knew that when he called the angel, somehow the angel showed up. Just as he did for all the Hearst brothers ever since he'd made them Guardians.

Inside the tunnel, he made his way to the roots of the tree. He paused at the threshold of golden knots of wood in the shapes of tiger and eagle. He held his wrist beneath a pointed root and waited for the drip of sap, the anointing ritual that joined him with his tree. In his impatience, it seemed to take forever, but at last, Custos recognized Aidan with a drop of amber sap onto his tattoo.

"Benison," he whispered, feeling the power of the oak.

"Benison," the tree replied.

It hadn't been long ago that he'd conferred with his brothers over the changing tide of the Dark Realm. Since the one hundred days before the Age of Atonement had begun, all evil forces were scrambling for change, to find the best position from which to win redemption they didn't deserve. Theodora was one of those forces. He knew he should've told his brothers what happened as soon as Theodora had appeared again, but since Rhianna had shown up, he'd been a bit preoccupied. He didn't even want to think about the earful they would give him. Maybe if he could fix it before they found out, they would take it easier on him.

He wound his way through the intricate halls of roots, down into the catacomb of knowledge. If there was a way to get to Riam without Theodora's "help," Custos would know.

Aidan sat on slab of polished wood. "I need your help, my friend," he said to the tree. "We need to bring Rhianna back to this dimension."

"That may not be possible. However, Theodora must be stopped," the tree's voice echoed, mixing with the sound of leaves rustling in the wind.

"You have knowledge of all the universe," Aidan said. "What can you tell be about Riam? How can I get there? How can I bring Rhianna back?"

Custos sighed. Aidan sensed the tree's hesitation, but he didn't know if it was the tree searching for the answer or trying to decide whether to help or not. One thing Aidan had learned over the years, though, was that one didn't rush a Divine Tree. So he waited as calmly as he could, hoping that Rhianna was unharmed and that he could soon find her.

It had seemed like hours had passed when the Divine Tree finally spoke. "Guardian, there is only one way to enter this universe, and that is to have Theodora transport you there, just as she does all her targets."

Ah shit. He scrubbed his face with his hand. "Why would she take me, though? How can I make her?"

Custos gave a dry laugh. "You must use cunning with her, not force."

Aidan growled low in his throat. "And to return?" he asked.

"You must relieve her of her power sources," Custos said. "What Theodora wants is more people and more property. Although the latter she can't actually do anything about. She's driven by greed and power. It bothers her that her world is so small compared to life on earth."

Aidan closed his eyes and examined his heart to determine if this woman was truly worth this journey.

Yes. Dammit. Yes.

"You rang?" Seth asked from behind Aidan.

Aidan flinched and spun around. "Must you sneak up on people?"

Seth chuckled, shrugged, and tucked his wings to his sides. "It's fun." His dreadlocks flipped forward over his shoulder.

"Right." Aidan stared at him, catching a whiff of garlic. "Geez, where have you been? You reek."

A smile split Seth's lips. "Brandt was having a party. That Brazilian food?" He kissed his fingertips and let them fly from his lips. "Mmm, so good. Now what's up?"

"I have a sorceress who's getting too big for her britches. Will you guard the tree while I get her back under control?"

"Well, I don't know. I have a manicure scheduled on Tuesday." He made a clicking sound in his cheek.

Aidan's glare bore into the angel. "I'm serious."

Seth crossed his arms. "Why now?"

"With the AOA upon us, we need to keep evil being under control, don't we?" Aidan said, not wanting to admit the truth.

"There's also a woman," Custos added with a raspy laugh.

Okay, so Aidan wouldn't have to admit it himself.

Seth gawked at Aidan. "Not you too."

"No, it's not like that," Aidan said with conviction. His brothers Venn and Ian had recently taken mates so he understood Seth's reference, but his situation was entirely different. This woman was in danger because of his island.

Holding up both hands, Seth backed up a few steps. "Okay. I'll watch the tree while you're away. Just don't be too long."

Aidan nodded. "Gotcha."

Seth raised a brow. "Gotcha? Really? You've been watching too many movies."

Waving off Seth, Aidan asked the tree, "Custos, is there anything else you can tell me about Riam?"

A rustle of leaves and branches rippled through the tree as if Custos were searching for something deep within. "You already know all you need to know."

Thirty minutes later, Aidan stood at the very spot where Rhianna had disappeared. He figured proximity may work in his favor. He wanted Theodora to think he was vulnerable and ripe for the picking.

Of course, *he was*. His emotions had become entangled with Rhianna somehow. He swallowed. What if he wasn't good enough, strong enough, or smart enough to bring her back? What if Theodora figured out that Rhianna was his Achilles' heel?

But first things first. He had to summon her. He didn't know how she knew where to appear and when, but maybe that orb on her scepter was like a crystal ball that helped her find the right place at the right time.

He said her name ever so softly, almost seductively, hoping she would hear him. "Theodora."

The ground and rocks shifted and churned, as if earth mover machinery was turning up the soil and trees in a continual motion. Theodora floated through the roiling mess, stopping in front of him.

"How can you help me?" she asked, a sneer of a smile pulling her lips to the side at her twist of words.

"Exactly," Aidan said. "I have some information I'm willing to exchange for—"

"I'm not bringing her back," she bit out.

"I'm not asking you to. I'm offering to go to your universe. You and I are not so different. We're both confined to our own small spaces. Me, to my tree and island. You, to Riam."

He was playing a game of poker right now, of course, and he had a good hand but not a perfect one. It was not an unbeatable hand; she could still best him. So he needed to be prepared to bluff really well.

Her eyes narrowed, suspicious. "Why? Why would you want to come with me?"

He shrugged. "I've been a Guardian for over eight hundred years. It's time for a change. Like you, I want more. I want more excitement. More than sitting by the tree and watching the years pass."

She smirked. "That pretty face got to you."

He didn't think the sorceress was capable of true feelings, but if she thought she could manipulate him, that might work in his favor. So he appealed to the instinct she would understand: greed.

"Perhaps," he said.

"What's in it for me?"

He lifted his chin and stared straight at her. "I have a secret of the Divine Tree I'm willing to share if you take me to Riam."

She shifted her stance. He could tell she was going to take the bait.

"Give it to me now," she purred.

He shook his head. "Oh no. I get there in one piece first."

Instead of being insulted, she smiled. With a swirl of her scepter, a porthole opened. Next, she locked him in a bubble, and for a second, panic rose within him as he tested his prison. The more he pushed, the tighter the confines became, so he relaxed and went with it. He only had one chance to get this right.

11

Aidan paid special attention as the porthole closed, the final snippet of the bubble disappearing into the scepter. Perhaps possessing the staff was the key to getting out.

He marked the terrain as he did in the ancient days in Scotland, noting a stand of three misshapen rocks on his left and tall sickly tree on his right. In the distance, there seemed to be city. He glanced at Theodora, who stood in the path of everything else, demanding his attention. Where was Rhianna? He tried to see around the sorceress.

"This is home sweet home from now on. Check in with the locals; they'll give you the rundown. You'll find them—and Rhianna—there." She pointed the scepter in the direction of the buildings. "Now, spill, Guardian. I believe you have something to tell me."

He stretched to his full height and crossed his arms. "I don't see her."

She shrugged. "She's around. Quit stalling."

"Okay. According to Custos"—he adopted a mysterious

tone and offered a lopsided smile—"zinc is the most important mineral in the world. It even keeps your skin looking young. You should try it."

She bared her teeth. "You lovesick fool. You traded your life for nothing. Nothing!" With her bare hands, she hurled a ball of energy at him that hit him square in the chest. The shot would have knocked out an average human. Good thing he was immortal, with great strength, stamina, and powers. He merely dropped to one knee, caught his breath, and then stood to face her once more.

The look on her face was priceless as she realized he was not going to respond the way normal men did. Her face reddened, enraged, and she rose into the air. Then, as if considering the matter, a wicked laugh peeled from her lips. "Actually, this is going to be most entertaining." She laughed again and disappeared.

Letting go of the tension holding him together, he doubled over in a coughing fit. Damn, that hurt. He rubbed his chest. Theodora got off on seeing people suffer, so he'd held it together to spite her. He straightened his spine and rotated his shoulders, still feeling the effect of hit.

He examined his surroundings with trepidation. Everything was gray and monochrome, totally devoid of color. There was no sunshine, either. Instead the sky was covered in a layer of clouds that seemed to suck the color out of everything.

He focused on the buildings along the horizon. He didn't see any cars or traffic, although he had not really expected to. Actually, he didn't even see any people, which was strange. Everything was still, dusty, and desolate.

Determined to find Rhianna and then a way out of here, he trekked toward the city. He passed a copse of trees and then shrubs, but they were dead, comprised of only brittle, gray leaves.

His boots stirred up dry, sooty earth as he walked. The

ground appeared to be made of volcanic rock. Abruptly, he froze. His eagle could fly to the city. Then a nerve-racking fear sliced through him. What if he couldn't change in this world? What if it didn't work and resulted in the crippling of limbs? He'd heard of alternate universes where the rules were different. Where powers didn't necessarily translate. There was a great deal he didn't know about Riam.

He ran a hand through his hair and cupped the base of his neck, weighing his options.

A glimpse of the very beginning of his time as a Guardian flashed through his mind, when he'd first learned of his shape-shifting powers and had tested them. The control had been something he'd had to grow into and learn over time. He imagined that in a new place there would be new rules. Would he have to start all over again?

Summoning his eagle, he focused on the change. His wings materialized agonizingly slow, and a twinge of nerves invaded his stomach. The restructuring of muscle and bone was painful, in a way like overstretching, pulling to the point of coming undone. He bit down on his lip. His mouth filled with the bitter, coppery taste of blood as his talons formed and his head morphed.

After a minute or so, the shift was complete. Shit, he hoped it was easier to change back to his human form. Yet, even with his concern, a thrill zinged through him as he took flight.

He soared a couple of miles and approached two gas stations, one on each side of the road. The signs above them were nondescript—HILLS GAS on one side and FALCONS on the other. The closer he got, the more his feathers stood on the back of his neck. Still, there was no one in sight.

How was he going to find Rhianna? Would she have entered the world in the same spot as he had? Had she passed by this place, too? Could she be inside, waiting?

The thought of what she must be feeling tore at his heart. As if she hadn't already experienced enough shock at learning who—and what—he was…

Something scuttled and scraped against the bricks of the Falcon station, or so it sounded like. He circled back toward the noise. Whatever it was he couldn't see. He veered right to get another angle. Something was there.

A strange sound echoed from afar, reminding him of something he'd heard on television once: a metal door opening on a sinking submarine.

Below him, people started running into the streets, brandishing weapons, swords, poles, sticks, pitchforks, whatever they could find, it seemed. The violence and gore of ancient combat unfolded quickly. Again, he was reminded of his youth. Long ago he'd brandished such weapons, but it had been for a noble cause, to save his lands from being overtaken. He wondered what the reason was behind this fighting.

Aidan glanced to his left, and then he understood. The sound he had heard must have been the signal to fight. It was a sick game. The question was, what were the rules?

He flew the length of the city and then back, his gaze sweeping the crowd, looking for Rhianna. The place looked like a war zone in the Middle East with dilapidated buildings and clutter along the streets. As he came around the Falcon station once more, he saw her.

A man pushed her into the street. "Fight. Fight," he yelled, instructing her to join in the fray.

She turned as a sword descended on the man next to her, slicing off his weapon hand. "Dillon!" she screamed.

The name seemed vaguely familiar. Then he recalled Rhianna had said it while recording on her GoPro. He must be one of her colleagues from the ship. Theodora had captured them all? *Damn.*

Aidan dove toward Rhianna, trying to keep her back,

even as the stranger grabbed hold of her arm. "Believe me, he'll want to die."

Rhianna tugged away from him. "What's happening? Why are they fighting?"

The man on the other side thrust his sword into Dillon's chest. Rhianna drew her hand to her mouth. "Oh God."

Aidan winged to a position between the Rhianna and the man, and then stretched out his wings, growing in size and towering over the guy as well as blocking Rhianna's view of the carnage. The man stumbled backward. One by one, the fighters ceased their attacks and their heads turned toward him. When everything was still, Aidan resumed his normal size and flew to Rhianna.

The people nearest to him in the crowd turned their heads to watch him.

"Aidan," she whispered, extending her arm. He landed on it.

Looks of awe swept across the faces in the crowd. They took a step back almost as a whole. Perhaps there were no birds in the place—or at least none with the ability to triple in size. He peered at Rhianna. Her jaw was set and she stood up straight, giving her a regal appearance.

A rumble passed through the ranks. These were the poor souls Theodora had collected over the centuries, the travelers who had ended up in a different destination from what they'd intended just because they'd entered the Dragon Vortex.

"We must hurry," one burly man said. The people gathered their injured and disappeared into the buildings like ants into a hill.

Rhianna turned, and three other men moved with their group around to the back of the Falcon station. The man who had been urging Rhianna to fight hustled away.

Aidan relaxed a fraction as he watched the guy's back as he ran.

As soon as their group rounded the corner. Aidan reverted to his human form.

She threw her arms around him. "I knew it was you."

He dragged her up against him and kissed her, hard and long, with all the pent-up frustration he'd been holding in check. Jesus, she felt so right in his arms.

"Whoa," the lanky man next to her said.

"It's okay," she said. "Sean, this is Aidan Hearst. Sole resident of Tsuriairando Island."

Sean bowed slightly at the waist. *"Aete ureshī yo,"* he said in Japanese.

"Pleased to meet you, too." Aidan matched his bow.

"Sean is our helicopter pilot."

Aidan nodded. It was nice to meet people from Rhianna's life. But he still had to get them out of there.

12

Theodora floated into town on Game Day as she usually did, but this time she was thoroughly ticked off. Actually, she had been since leaving that Guardian on the road. And now the game had ended short. She expelled a huff of air. It didn't matter; she hadn't been watching anyway.

The leaders of the two factions she's created—Mamushi and Habu—presented their dead for the tally. She scanned the crowd, glaring. "Really, people. This is a pitiful showing. It's as if your hearts aren't in the game."

She counted the bodies. Mamushi team won with seventeen kills. She slid the prize bucket of extra food and blankets to their side of street. The men and women hurriedly scooped items up, hugging them tight to their chests, and scampered into the building.

"Habu team, I've got nothing for you." She laughed. She loved saying that line, loved seeing their faces fall.

With a swirl of her scepter, the dead were healed and put back together. The group moaned in pain as they became whole again, an added delight to seeing them die over and over again.

"You need to do better next time or there will be a penalty. Got it?" She didn't wait for anyone to answer. They knew better than that. So she just vanished in a puff of red smoke.

Each side gathered their men and women and disappeared back into the buildings.

Aidan ducked through the unhinged doorway of the Falcon gas station, keeping Rhianna close to him, almost blocking her from view in case Theodora were to return. He wondered if she could find them anyway. Probably. But that wasn't something he'd dwell on now.

Now that they were concealed within the station, Rhianna leaned against him. He wrapped an arm around her shoulders and hugged her. Thank god she was safe.

Three men entered, two of them supporting Dillon Savage by his arms as he stumbled through the doorway. They were all breathing hard, all seeming to still be in shock. Which was understandable. They had just witnessed—hell, been a part of—an ancient war game. The only difference was that the fallen were brought back to life, the epitaph of the phrase "live to fight another day."

Aidan combed Rhianna's hair back with his fingers, searching her face. "Are you all right? Any injuries?"

"I'm fine. Just a few bruises," she answered. She rested against him for a minute and then stepped back, looking at the other men. "Aidan, this is Steve and Dillon from the TV show. You already met Sean." She paused a beat, her expression shifting from relieved to one of concern. "Are you guys okay?"

They nodded and grumbled.

"So it plays out like a video game for her entertainment," Aidan muttered.

"I guess. This was our first time," Steve said, agitated.

"She took us from our ship and dropped us here," Sean explained. "We had no idea what was going on. But the people here are quick to tell you. And if you look at their necks, there are marks that indicate how many times they've died and been brought back. Evidently, 'Game Day' takes place once a week."

Dillon's gaze darted around frantically. "That sucks." He finally released his death grip on his sword and let it drop to the ground. He rubbed his wrist. Blood stained his clothes. "I've... I've never seen anything like it."

"At least you have another chance to live and find a way out of here," Aidan said.

Dillon nodded as he pressed his lips together, clearly trying not to lose it. He hung his head and folded his arms in against his body.

Steve looked off in the distance. "Is there a way out of this hellhole?" he asked.

With a heavy sigh, Dillon pulled himself straighter. "The poor son of a bitches have to go through this over and over. You can't believe how painful it is to die and wake up. No wonder they become expert fighters. The best don't get killed."

Rhianna pulled away from him suddenly and looked up at him, confused. "Wait. What are you doing here?" she asked.

"I came to get you out," Aidan said. "Any ideas?" He was trying to lighten the mood, but it wasn't something he was very skilled at.

Rhianna didn't smile, but tears glazed her eyes. "Thank you," she said. "No. Just know we gotta get out of here," Rhianna said.

Dillon rubbed his temple. "I'm tired."

"Look," she said to Aidan, pointing at Dillon's neck. "A black mark. Like Steve said."

Aidan squinted at the tiny slash. "Some of the people had them all the way around their throats in rows."

Dillon closed his eyes, his face full of anguish.

"Poor devils," Steve said.

Indeed. He wouldn't want to endure that over and over again. He turned his gaze to Rhianna. Her hair was disheveled and her cheeks smudged with dirt. None of these people should have to stay here, but his number one concern was getting Rhianna out.

He glanced around still trying to put the pieces of the puzzle together that made up this absurd game of Theodora's.

"How do you know what team you're on?" Aidan asked.

"This side of the road is Mamushi; the other is Habu," Steve said.

"Huh, she named them after snakes." Anxious to come up with a plan, Aidan paced around the group.

"Yeah, I remember the mamushi from our safety literature," Steve added. "Its bite causes the tissue to liquefy. The victim literally loses a chunk of his body." He scrunched his face and shook his head. "Ugh."

Rhianna shuddered. "I hate snakes."

Aidan paused, allowing his thoughts to solidify into a plan. "Steve, Sean, and Dillon, see what information you can learn about these games? Is there anything else we need to know? Rhianna, you stay put and get some rest. I'm going on a reconnaissance flight to see how big this universe is and come up with a plan to escape."

"What is he talking about," Dillion asked Rhianna. Still dazed from what he'd been through.

Rhianna rested a hand on Dillion's shoulder. "He has some special abilities. Just trust him."

"Whatever you do, promise to take us with you," Dillon begged.

"We're all going to get out of here," Aidan promised.

"I'm with you," Steve assured him. "Thanks."

"I'm sure all the people here feel the same," Sean added.

Rhianna sucked in a breath, placing her hand on his arm. "Oh my god. What if my great-grandfather is here?" She shook her head, as if scolding herself. "Why wasn't that the first thing I thought of?"

"Don't count on it," Aidan muttered without thinking.

Her lips turned down and her eyes misted. A pained look crossed her face.

He wished he could take the words back. "I'm sorry. I didn't mean to be harsh. I just don't want you to get your hopes up. Your great-grandfather has been gone a long time, and he must be quite old now."

And I'm a boor who isn't used to dealing with people.

He stepped closer to her and drew her into his arms, stroking her silky hair. She rested her cheek against his chest. "But I'll still do my best to find him."

Her response was to squeeze him tighter around his middle and snuggle into him.

His heart skipped several beats. He'd give anything to make her happy. Anything.

13

Anxiety gnawed at Aidan as he took flight. He needed to find a way out, yet he hated leaving Rhianna behind. The skies were the same as when he'd arrived—gray and overcast. He began at his entrance point and glided around the perimeter. The universe seemed to have definite boundaries but no fixed compass. It was comprised of the city, a valley, and a mountain range where there was a partially hidden fortress. Where Theodora lived, he figured.His primary duty was to the tree. He needed to let Death know he was up against his ultimate opponent. He would not be weakened by a woman, the death of a human, or any other circumstance. He was a Guardian first and foremost.

He landed near a tree and shifted to his human form. Hoping to discover some clue about the structure of this universe and its boundaries, he examined the area near where he'd entered. Unlike on his side, there was a distinct line where he couldn't progress farther. At that point, his hand disappeared into a fog and he felt resistance. It was not like a solid wall; it was similar to the elasticity of a balloon. He wondered if it could be penetrated.

He transformed into his tiger, unfurled his sharp claws and thrust his weight onto the boundary. As he forcefully dug in, the boundary shot him backwards. Still, he didn't give up. He charged forward time and again, hoping to create a weak area that he could pierce.

The boundary remained.

Frustrated and disheartened, after he'd checked everything he could think of, he tore across the gray ground expelling some of his anger, in his effort to return to Rhianna.

The men had all left, and Rhianna pushed herself away from the wall. While she should probably stay here so Aidan could find her, she had to find out if her great-grandfather was here.

Aidan would no doubt be awhile. She would just hurry.

Even though the people had said the wars were weekly, Rhianna had to forcefully tamp down her fear that another war session would start unexpectedly. It had been too traumatic, and she didn't trust Theodora. What if the sorceress changed the rules?

Rhianna hustled through the streets, asking all the passersby if they knew Katsu Mori. Never in her wildest dreams would she have imagined this could be where her great-grandfather had gone, that he could be alive. Yes, he would be elderly, but who was to say Theodora didn't bring back those who died of old age or natural causes back to life? She did it with all those killed in battle, after all.

Rhianna thought of her grandfather at home. He might be going through his Tai Chi exercises right now. She recalled her last visit, when she'd promised him she'd do her best to discover what happened to his father.

With a sigh, she set her jaw resolutely. She could fulfill one dream, even if it was her last one. She could try to find her great-grandfather. If he was taken to this alternate world all that time ago, she felt certain he would be here now.

She snagged the wrist of the next person she passed. "Sir, do you know someone named Katsu Mori?" she asked.

The man eyed her warily. "Yes, I have heard of him. But I'm not sure where he lives."

Her eyes widened, and her heart began to race. He might really be there!

"You may want to try the library," he added. "Some people hang out there. Someone there might know something."

She looked to where he was pointing. "Thank you!" she called as she ran toward the library building. She shoved the door open and rushed inside. The shelves around her were less than half full, but she was pleased to find that the stranger had been right: there were more than twenty people sitting in a huddle of sorts.

Rhianna knelt down to join the group and noticed the marks on their necks. She swallowed. "How long have you been here?" she asked the blond man nearest her.

"Since 1952," he replied.

A woman with red hair leaned forward. "1820. I was sailing from Alaska, traveling to Russia to see my mother," she explained, her voice bitter. "I never made it. This is where I ended up.

"I've been here since 2002," a twentysomething man chimed in.

Rhianna's brow furrowed. She couldn't help but notice that they had not only come to this place at different times but they were all different ages; however, none of them were really looked very *old*. It was as if they had not aged.

And if that one woman had been here since the nineteen hundreds… Rhianna shook her head. It wasn't possible. But then a lot of things she'd thought were impossible were apparently real.

"What is happening in the world now?" the young man asked.

Rhianna licked her lips. She didn't have much time, but she offered the guy two quick pieces of information he might relate to. "Donald Trump is president of the United States, and the Mars One is planning to establish a settlement on Mars in 2024."

The young man smiled and nodded, his eyes looking glassy and sad.

"Have you heard of someone by the name of Katsu Mori?" she inquired then, taking a few steps away, preparing to move on if no one knew.

Several people nodded, but it was the young man who replied. "When you live in a community of around four hundred people, you know almost everyone. That's what makes fighting so hard."

"And Katsu?" She paused, tilting her head and smiling. "What of him?"

"He is one of the leaders. I will take you to him," an older man said as he stood up.

She inhaled sharply, her chest pounding as if fireworks were going off in her heart. She thanked the others and then hurried after the man.

She exited the building to find Aidan marching toward her. He pulled her aside. "What are you doing here?"

His tone irritated her at first, but then the knot in her stomach eased. She hadn't realized how tense she had been. Just having him near gave her comfort. If only he weren't being so overbearing.

She rested her palm on his chest. "I'm collecting information," she said matter-of-factly. "What about you? Did you discover anything?"

He glanced at the man beside her. "Yes. I'll tell you when we get back to the station."

"Well, I may have struck pay dirt." She smiled up at him. She looked to the man who was helping her and smiled at him, too.

Her escort didn't seem too pleased that Aidan had joined them, though. He backed away from them, saying, "Maybe we should do this later."

"No." Aidan flashed a grin, obviously trying to charm the man. "I only want to help."

Slowly, the man stepped forward. "Katsu is usually at his home. This way."

She didn't know if any of these buildings could truly be considered a home, but she didn't care. She just wanted to find her great-grandfather.

Aidan slipped his hand behind her back as they walked. She leaned into him, savoring his touch. At least that was something real that she could hold on to, unlike the rest of this...this...make-believe world. She was at a loss of how else to think about this place.

When they made their way halfway across town the man stopped in front of a small building that had no door in the frame and no windows to be seen. "This is it," he said. "If he's not here, then I don't know where he is."

"Thank you," she said. "I appreciate your help."

Her guide left, and she reached across to take Aidan's hand in hers. "I'm nervous."

"After all that's happened, *this* is what makes you uneasy?" He gave her a half smile, obviously trying to calm her.

She shrugged. Everything else that had happened hadn't had expectations attached to it. It had all been a flat-out shock and surprise. But her great-grandfather... She'd wanted to know about him for as long as she could remember. Her palms grew moist, and her breathing turned shallow.

Aidan squeezed her hand. "Have courage."

She closed her eyes, took a deep breath, and nodded.

Once she opened them again, Aidan slapped his hand against the entry wall. "Hello?"

They walked slowly inside, stopping at the inner doorway. A man sat cross-legged in the center of the room, his head dipped down. He appeared to be meditating.

"Katsu Mori?" she whispered.

"How may I help you?" he said without lifting his head, his eyes closed.

Rhianna shuffled forward. "I don't mean to interrupt your meditation."

"Yet you have." He looked up, raised an eyebrow but then smiled.

Aidan came up beside her.

"You are Katsu Mori, yes?" she asked quietly, squatting.

He lifted his head a little more, seaming curious at her question. She glimpsed a single row of black marks now visible on his neck. He hadn't died very many times considering how long he'd been there.

"I am," he said.

"I am the daughter of Akira Mori, who is the son of Shirō Mori...your son." She sat back on her heels and waited for his response.

A double blink of his eyelids was the only sign of his surprise.

"I believe I am your great-granddaughter," she said.

If she had expected a show of fanfare at her announcement, what she got was far from it. The lines on his face tugged downward. "It saddens me that you are here."

"You do not wish to see me?" Her heart sank, especially after all she'd withstood before coming here, to get to this point.

"I do not wish for you to endure this endless life." His eyes lacked any spark or joy as he spoke.

Aidan eased forward. "We intend to escape this place. Do you have any information that might help us?"

"Meditate. It is the only means of escape."

"We're after something a lot more permanent," Aidan said.

"Then I cannot help you," Katsu retorted. "If there was a way out, I would have found it years ago."

"What of the boundary. When I found it, it seemed flexible," Aidan said, surprising her. He hadn't yet had a chance to tell her what he'd found out. "Can it be pierced?"

Katsu shook his head ever so slightly. "No one has ever left."

Rhianna averted her eyes and swallowed hard as disappointment fanned in her chest. She tried to control her breathing as she fought her emotions.

Don't cry.

"What about Theodora? What is her weakness?" Rhianna straightened her spine as the idea materialized. "Maybe if we stole her scepter! It seems to be the source of her power. Surely that would get us out."

Katsu's eyes met hers for the first time. "No one has accomplished that, either. And Theodora is a master of torture." He glanced to Aidan and back to her. "It will not work. Do not try it."

Disillusionment and frustration flooded her. She wondered what sort of torture he spoke of and how he knew. Her gaze slid to Aidan. She didn't want to see anyone she loved be put to the test.

Tears rolled down her cheeks. She held her face in her hands. "I'm sorry. I'm tired...and...and I never imagined this world existed, let alone feared being here."

Aidan eased her up and put his strong arms around her, holding her to him. "I'll find a way. I promise."

"But you're on the right track in one respect," Kastu said. "Any answer lies with the sorceress." He stared intensely at Aidan, as if trying to impart a message.

Rhianna glanced between the two men. Were they exchanging some sort of communication? Could there be more to Aidan's powers than she knew?

14

Aidan escorted Rhianna back to the Falcon station, which had become their home base. She was stumbling as they went, and he supported her with his arm beneath her ribs.

He was worried about her. She needed rest and food to keep going. And she'd had little of either since Theodora had seized her yesterday.

"You need to rest, just for a little while," he said to Rhianna.

She shook her head weakly. "I can't sleep. There's too much at stake. We only have six days before the next Game Day." She groaned. "And that's only if Theodora sticks to the same schedule she's been using."

"Two hours," he pleaded. "We won't lose that much for you to catch a two-hour nap."

She pulled away from him. "Nope."

When they got inside the station, it was empty. Steve, Sean, and Dillon hadn't returned. He plopped onto the sofa and patted the worn, faded cushion. "Have a seat," he said. "They'll probably be back any minute."

"Do you think they are all right?" she asked, furrowing her brow.

"Sure. They were here before you, right?"

She sat by his side and, with his guidance, rested her head on his shoulder. Her cinnamon scent filled his nostrils. Her softness teased his fingertips, and he listened as her breathing relaxed and slowed. She fell asleep within minutes.

Having her there beside him felt so right. He couldn't believe he'd lived his immortal life alone. And while she would sadly be more or less immortal now, this was not a life. He wanted so much more for her—love, joy, laughter.

Rhianna slept for perhaps an hour and a half and then woke with a jerk. She moaned and clutched him tighter as she flung her arms around his ribs.

He dipped his head and gently kissed her. "Any other time, and I'd make love to you." His lips tugged on hers and his tongue traced the inside of her mouth. They groaned in unison. "I promise you, we'll continue this another day. When we're free of this place."

He cradled her against his chest again and closed his eyes. She drifted off for a second time. He didn't sleep, though, but his mind ran through potential scenarios for how to get them out of this before the next Game Day.

Awhile later, Steve and the others came shuffling in. Aidan pressed his index fingers to his lips. Rhianna was still sleeping.

Dillon nodded, and set a small plate of chicken and rice on the table. The guys each dropped into one of the mismatched chairs scattered around the room. Sean's seat slid and squeaked.

Aidan held his breath. Rhianna stirred but didn't wake.

He exhaled. *Good.* His job was to be a Guardian. He'd done it for hundreds of years, and now he needed to protect *her.*

He fisted his hands at his side. The weight of being alone for so long had finally been lifted, only to be replaced by the fear of losing Rhianna. He couldn't allow that to happen.

The passage of time was a strange thing without the normal rise and fall of the sun. Rhianna, along with the guys, dozed for a few hours, barely moving. But when she did, Aidan stroked her back to rouse her. He wanted to take a stab at the perimeter before the rest of the population stirred. If he found a way out, he felt compelled to return and help the others escape this torturous existence also.

"Rhianna, wake up," he nudged.

She kicked her leg over his waist, slid on top of him, and snuggled down into the sofa. He hissed in a breath. God, she felt so good.

But now was not the time, he reminded himself.

He jostled her. "Hey, we have to see if we can find a way out."

As she came awake, she sat abruptly, pushed off him, and stood in one motion. "You let me fall asleep," she accused him, her face turning red with fury. "Even after I told you I didn't want to."

He lifted both hands and shrugged. "You're not the only one." He jutted his chin to indicate the other three men, each sacked out on a chair, looking uncomfortable but dead to the world.

She waved a finger at him. "No. You knew perfectly well what I wanted and you disregarded it." She made a growling sound deep in her throat. "Look at the time we've wasted!"

He stood, ignoring the uneasy feeling in his chest, a

discomfort that worsened the angrier she got. He wasn't used to having a female mad at him. Part of him didn't know how to react.

Unable to resist and thinking this may be their final day together, he cupped her face with both hands and kissed her lovely lips. She tasted even better than he'd remembered. "If we get out of this…"

Her hands slid up to his biceps, where she dug her nails in, seeming unwilling to forgive him. Then her eyes flashed with lust, and she moved her palms to his chest and up to his jawline. She matched his movements and passionately kissed him back, tangling her tongue with his and finishing with a long, sensual pull on his lips.

They were both breathing hard. "That's *when*. When we get out of here. We *will* finish this." She met his gaze uttering nearly the same promise he'd said earlier.

He threaded his hand into her hair and brought her close for one more kiss. "Okay. *When*."

Dillon cleared his throat. "Now that that's settled, what's next?"

Aidan held on to Rhianna as he answered. "We head out."

"I know you're coming up with a plan," Dillon added. "Just wanted to make sure you include us."

"Yeah," Steve said, still groggy. "We'll help. Tell us what to do."

He turned away. "Sure." He stared at the guys, silently daring them to contradict him "Bring your weapons."

A few minutes later, he ushered everyone out the door, then paused. "I want to prepare you… If we encounter Theodora, it *will* get ugly. You don't have to go."

They looked around at one another.

"One corner of Hell is as bad as another," Dillon said. "I'm in."

Steve nodded.

"Damn right," Sean agreed.

"Okay," Aidan said. "Just don't expect me to save all your asses."

Although he knew it wasn't in him to leave a man behind.

It had taken them an hour or so to make it to where they had entered this pitiful world. She had a vague feeling that time may not pass the same in this world. So she couldn't be sure.

Whether they made it or not, she was thankful that he was trying. At least they were doing something other than waiting for the next Game Day. It gave her hope that they could do it, that they would get out of here.

"Hand me your sword," Aidan said to Rhianna. She held it out to him as he pushed on the elastic wall with his hand. Once he was holding the hilt of the sword, he nudged the barrier with the tip of the blade. He hesitated.

"What's wrong?" she asked.

He pressed his lips together. "I'm just wondering what will happen if I *can* slice through the barrier. Will it lead us out of Riam and directly to our world? Or does it lead elsewhere?"

"At this point, it doesn't matter. It's the only option we have," she said with a frown.

No, he thought, *it's the first option we have.*

And the easiest. But it was worth testing the theory because other options involved confronting Theodora face-to-face, which was a far more dangerous prospect.

Steve stepped toward them. "What do you think will happen? Perhaps it will exhale us like a balloon does air."

"Whatever occurs—" Aidan's brows came together and he scowled at the men "—we get Rhianna out. If something happens to me...*you* get Rhianna out. Understood?"

The three men nodded. "Understood."

Aidan thrust the sword into the fog that hovered around the barrier. The steel bounced off the elastic structure, almost flying out of his hand.

"Try it slowly," Rhianna said. "You might be able to use the point to tear it."

Aidan did as she suggested and pushed it slowly this time, his bicep bulging with the effort. He twisted the sword, pushed harder, and then tried again. But the invisible barrier still did not yield.

A hissing female laugh made all four of them turn. "Well, well. What have we here?"

Dillon literally shook in his boots, Steve's mouth gaped open, and Sean threw his arm over his eyes.

Aidan stepped to the front of the group. "I had to at least try."

"Of course you did." She gave a wicked laugh as she hurled fireballs at him in quick succession. He made quick work of deflecting them all, but it took a toll on him.

Rhianna grabbed his arm as he stumbled, exhausted.

"Oh, gag me," Theodora said, eyeing Aidan and Rhianna. Producing another magical net with her staff, she locked the five of them in it and floated them back to the city.

Aidan cut at the net with Rhianna's sword, but it held strong. Everything she used had magical properties. How did he fight that?

Then a bronze chariot pulled by six black horses materialized out of thin air. Theodora hurled the net in the back and flew into the city with great fanfare.

Instead of being mad, she seemed quite pleased, as if she was utterly entertained by this change of events and their attempt to flee.

Oh God. What did she have in store for them now?

15

Aidan's arms ached from pushing on the confines of the net to make more room so as not to crush Rhianna. The invisible trap hugged the five of them tightly, and he worked it so she would at least be on top.

Theodora placed them on display in the center of town, hanging the net from a large hook that extended from the facade of the library. She had obviously done this before. Now more than ever, Katsu's comment about torture niggled at Aidan.

The people didn't come out of the dwellings, but he could see their eyes watching from behind the windows. A few heads extended beyond doorways, then quickly ducked back inside.

"Sharpen your weapons. At five o'clock, there will be an extra special Game Day," Theodora announced.

Aidan fisted his hands. "Theodora, how about something a bit different? Why don't you just pit me against your best fighter? I'm certain it would be a good show."

He'd expected some form of retribution for their attempt to escape, but he was worried about Rhianna. He needed to shift the sorceress's attention.

"I don't give a damn about *their* entertainment," Theodora bit out. "I will not be deserted. You should not have tried to leave." Her voice had a insane quality to it.

He put his lips beside Rhianna's ear and whispered, "If we fight, stay behind me. And if you *must* fight, position yourself around those who have many marks on their neck. They will be the weakest. With your fighting skills, you will do well." He attempted to build her confidence. It might be the only thing she had going for her.

She glanced sideways at him. "Okay."

He let his lips brush her cheek. He didn't want her to fight at all, dammit. A fire started to burn in his gut at his helplessness.

Theodora took a position on a terrace in the middle of the square. She waved a hand. A strange, eerie sound echoed along the street, it was like a high-pitched horn, signaling the fight to begin. Then her voice boomed. "Kill the Guardian and you earn an extra boon!"

Aidan wondered how the people would know he was a Guardian. Then he recalled that he'd transformed into his eagle form during the last war.

Theodora lifted her scepter, the net vanished, and the five of them dropped to the ground. Aidan landed on his feet and helped Rhianna up from the ground. A cloud of dirt swirled around them, getting in his eyes and making Rhianna cough. He pushed her behind him as he heard the battle cries of the people.

Men and women alike burst from the buildings, converging on them but clearly aiming for him. Which was good, he thought. It would take the pressure off Rhianna.

One man in particular caught his attention as he rushed toward them with a samurai sword—Rhianna's great-grandfather. Katsu positioned himself next to Rhianna. She nodded at him and assumed a fighting stance, her feet wide apart, one foot forward, and the other back to easily shift her weight.

Her great-grandfather wielded his sword, taking down any opponent that came near Rhianna. When there were so many he couldn't fend them all off, one slipped through. Rhianna was ready, though, and she swung around in a karate jump, fanning her leg and knocking her attacker off his feet. Katsu finished the man off with a clean stab to the heart.

Six men charged at Aidan then. With a bend and jump, he shifted into his tiger form. The change was enough to throw the fighters off guard and cause them to hesitate. He leaped over them and burst into a full run. Men darted into his path, swinging their swords, striking wildly as he passed, hoping to do damage. He roared, bared his teeth, and dodged each attack.

Out of the corner of his eye, he kept watch on Theodora and the scepter. If they were going to get out of here, that was the key.

He sprinted for the elevated terrace from where she observed the battle.

Theodora watched him approach. His great paws thudded over the ground as he got closer and closer. Her gaze slid back to the fighting.

"The woman! Kill the woman!" Theodora ordered her subjects.

Aidan looked back. "No!" he screamed.

But the crowd didn't hesitate, and they shifted their attack. Katsu slashed every opponent that came within range of his blade. But two men with bloodlust on their eyes got past. Rhianna hit them hard, using her karate and weapons training, but one man spun clear of her kick and struck her down with a blow to the side of her neck. It was enough to topple her. Rhianna fell, blood seeping from the wound, and her eyes rolled back into her head as it hit the ground.

A roar ripped from Aidan's throat, so violent that the taste of blood invaded his mouth. A throbbing pain squeezed his chest at her unmoving body, an ache he couldn't bear racking through him. Focusing all of his abilities on her, he tried to distinguish her heartbeat.

Nothing. A volcano of agony erupted inside of him. He had lost her before he had ever truly had her.

He used all his rage and anguish to vault himself off the dais, transforming into his eagle and launching into flight. He soared, and soared, and soared, trying to push past the agony to think clearly. He couldn't make an attempt for the scepter now. He had to wait until Theodora brought Rhianna back to life. So what did he do now?

Another fear hit him. Would the sorceress even bring her back?

16

Soaring above the crowd, Aidan held his breath as he
watched. All of the people who had gone with him to the
barrier were dead, including his beloved Rhianna. He flew
to the highest perch at the top of the library to watch and
wait as the leaders gathered their dead.

Katsu carried Rhianna. A sharp pain stabbed at Aidan's
heart seeing her limp body in her great-grandfather's arms.

Aidan was afraid to breathe or move. What if Theodora
decided not to revive them this time? What if she chose to
keep Rhianna from him forever to get back at him?

He ground his teeth at the thought, trying to restrain
himself from going down there and demanding Theodora
release Rhianna from the grip of death.

Theodora made a show before her players, bringing the
warriors back to life. The tension in Aidan's chest eased.
She was doing it. He would get another chance with
Rhianna, another chance to get her out of Riam.

The sorceress set down her scepter when there were

only four bodies left unmoving on the ground—Dillon, Steve, Sean, and Rhianna. All the pain rushed back into his body as Theodora's eyes searched the crowd him, probably for him, he knew. Would she make them pay just to twist the knife in his gut? Of course she would. He turned and flew down the street, intending to present a devil-may-care attitude, just as he had essentially done for years when she'd stole people from his island. He hadn't known then what this life was like for them. A living hell.

The guilt set in. He had ignored all those poor people...

He didn't know how he could have stopped her, but he could have at least made it a lot harder and perhaps not worth her while. Not on his island, anyway.

At last Theodora waved the staff, breathing life back into the three men. They rolled on the ground, groaning in their agony.

Sometimes pain is good, he thought. *It means you are alive.*

Then Theodora shot him a piercing stare and hesitated. His breath caught. She had to bring back Rhianna. She *had* to.

Pointing the scepter toward Rhianna, Theodora called out to Katsu. "Old man." He looked up silently, as if waiting for further instruction. "Bring the girl to my palace."

Katsu nodded, though Aidan could see the man's clenched jaw and the sadness in his eyes. Rhianna remained unconscious as he carried her down the road. He disappeared into the woods, following the long trail that led to Theodora's castle in the mountains.

Theodora must have been pleased with herself, her voice raised in jubilant eagerness as she announced, "A bonus for all!"

Immediately, a long table appeared down the length of the street. It was piled high with food in one long horn-of-plenty: platers of roast beef, lamb, ham, and poultry, with every sort of fruit and vegetable imaginable.

The people stepped back with hesitation, their eyes

wide. When they realized this feast was meant for them the scene turned into a mob attacking the food both eating and storing what they could. A man removed his shirt to create a make-shift satchel. Other's stuffed pocket and hats with goods.

Theodora peered straight over at where Aidan was perched, the challenge evident in her eyes. He read the message loud and clear...she was in control. Then she disappeared in a swirl of red smoke.

Aidan understood Theodora's taunt. She'd taken Rhianna because she assumed that he'd come after her.

And she was correct. He'd go beyond this dimension... and to the end of the earth for Rhianna.

His heart pounded in his head, making it hard to think as he soared to the mountain range. At first, he thought to intercept Katsu and Rhianna en route. But when he didn't encounter them, he realized Theodora must have already intervened and taken them to her palace.

He flew over the ridges, watching and ready. There was no telling what Theodora would do to stop him. She would not make it easy. That was part of the game. Yes, she expected him to follow her. He was only certain she would be ready for him. His first weapon to thwart her would be speed. If he could just get there before she locked him out—and he was sure she would—then he may have a chance.

He flew low, close to the treetops. As soon as he was within sight of the palace, he anticipated smashing into some sort of barricade or force she'd put up. What sort of trap had she laid for him?

But nothing happened as he approached. Perhaps he'd managed to get through before she'd set one up. Still, it made him nervous that he hadn't run into resistance yet. His back and shoulder muscles tensed as he pushed his wings into an extended glide. He glanced toward the woods and saw nothing.

When he looked forward again, he noticed a cloud of roiling red smoke was heading toward him, moving swiftly before overtaking and enveloping him. He couldn't see but a foot in front of him. Within seconds, he grew disoriented.

Panic began to set in. He couldn't fly blind. So he descended, going slowly, hoping not to face plant into a tree or cliff. As he landed, he wondered if that was Theodora's intent—to make him approach from the ground and not the air.

For now he called on his tiger to run and scale the high cliffs, maneuvering with the confidence of the big cat he was. The going proved much slower than flying, but thick red smoke still permeated everything. If he could find a trail up the mountain, the traveling would be easier.

He knew one thing for certain: the castle sat at the top of the mountain. So if he kept going up, he was heading in the right direction. Relying heavily on his sense of smell and his superhuman hearing, he crept silently through the shadows, allowing them to conceal him. He didn't actually expect Theodora to be in the woods, but he couldn't be positive, either.

Near the top of the mountain, he finally came upon a path and halted, peering across a gigantic ravine to where he thought Theodora's castle stood. He barely made out the suspended drawbridge and castle base on the other side. The rest of the structure vanished in the red fog.

Taking a moment to catch his breath, he stared at an empty space in the middle of the bridge making it look incomplete. He suspected the space only materialized due to some mystical persuasion from Theodora, so that whoever tried to cross would think it was impossible, or they would risk ending up at the bottom of the gorge.

He sighed, and then a scream split the air. Jerking his head up, he heard another high-pitched cry.

Rhianna!

He ran off the edge of the precipice and transformed from tiger to eagle. He plummeted at first, then caught the wind beneath his wings and rose.

It was only a short distance more to the castle, and the closer he got, the easier it was the see through the fog.

Once he was inside the palace, he'd have to find a way to get Theodora to bring Rhianna back to life and then destroy the sorceress. He didn't know how he would do that yet, what her weakness was, but he'd find one. And whatever it was, he'd use it against her.

Anxiety skipped along Rhianna's spine. Her palms were sweating profusely, and she could hardly focus. At least Theodora had allowed her great-grandfather to be the one who stayed to guard her.

"Don't worry," Katsu told her. "You will be fine."

Yeah, right. Easy for you to say.

She had died and been revived. To say she was shaken was an understatement. When air had filled her lungs again for the first time, she had screamed at the pain of it. But her great-grandfather had an easy way about him that reassured her.

"Aidan will be coming for me," she whispered to Katsu.

He nodded, a shadow of sadness crossing his face. "Rest," he said and then shut the door to her room. She felt his presence as he remained on the other side.

She inhaled several calming breaths before she turned and regarded the room. One thing was for sure: Theodora lacked an eye for beauty. Rhianna would have thought that there would have been some color in the sorceress's own palace, if nowhere else in this world. Perhaps there was something wrong with her eyes. Was she color-blind?

The bedroom she'd been escorted to had sturdy Baroque furniture and a plump bed. The accommodations were far superior to the bare room she'd been given in town. She drew back the covers and climbed beneath them. She stared at the high ceiling. And while her body was more comfortable now than it had been in days, a single tear slid down her cheek. She closed her eyes.

Sometime later Rhianna was awoken by the sound of a scrape and a thump. She jumped and snapped open her eyes. It took a moment for the shape at the end of her bed to come into focus.

Aidan.

She tucked her knees beneath her, scooted across the mattress, and threw herself into his open arms.

"Are you all right?" he asked, touching her face gently.

She nodded, then took in a deep breath of his comforting, manly scent. "How did you get in here?"

"I came in the window in another room. It was a tight squeeze, but I managed. Katsu directed me here."

"I guess my great-grandfather likes me more than I thought," she said, offering a grim smile.

"His indifferent nature is just due to the culture and age in which he lived. Remember, he's old, even though he doesn't look it."

She nodded again. She wanted to run away, to disappear beneath the covers with a book the way she had when she was small. "I wish I could forget all this. I wish we could be back at your island."

He lifted her chin and kissed her, the tender strength of his lips on hers giving her hope. "Come on. We must leave."

She tried to stand but pain shot through her body, and she stumbled.

"It's okay," he whispered. "Lean on me. I'll hold you up."

17

Aidan knew he needed to get Rhianna out of there. The problem was he didn't know where to go, nor how to get her there in her weakened state? He could carry her without a problem, but how would they hide from the sorceress? Or how could he challenge Theodora without putting Rhianna at risk to suffer the consequences.

He could take anything the sorceress doled out... anything except seeing Rhianna hurt.

He didn't want to push Rhianna too hard—she was human and had just been through a horrific experience. But something told him there was no time. He stepped from the bed and reached for his sword, forgetting it didn't travel with him when he shape-shifted.

Theodora threw open the door and charged inside. She touched the ring on her right hand and brandished the scepter at him. The sphere glowed white. It was the first time he'd seen it turn any color but blue. What did that mean?

Rhianna straightened in his arms, her expression stoic

despite the pain he knew she was in.

"I knew you would come for her," Theodora crooned.

Suddenly, the walls and floor of the room began to move. The individual bricks shifted and rotated, moving and shifting into different positions like a colorless kaleidoscope. Both he and Rhianna were thrown off-balance, knocking their shoulders together then falling to the floor. Rhianna landed on top of him as the room settled into what appeared to be a dungeon.

With her open palm extended toward Rhianna, Theodora picked her up and sent her sailing into another cell across the hallway. Rhianna slammed into the wall with a groan. The door shut with a loud *clack*, and a key magically turned to lock the door before floating into Theodora's hand.

Rhianna staggered to her feet and cursed as she ran to the door as best she could. She grasped the iron bars. "Let us out! Let us go home!" she yelled.

Theodora smiled, her lips peeling back from her teeth. "What's mine stays mine. Unless..." She paused and glanced back at Aidan, as if considering something. "Unless you're dead."

Aidan narrowed his eyes at Theodora. What was she going on about? More than tired of Theodora's games, he stood and charged after her, trying to grab the staff from her hands.

Theodora lunged forward and aimed the scepter at Rhianna. A lightning bolt shot from the orb and pierced Rhianna's chest. Her eyes rolled up in their sockets again as she collapsed—again—to the damp floor. Her heart had even stopped beating. Aidan's superhuman hearing could detect the silence.

"No!" Aidan shouted.

Theodora let Rhianna remain where she was, doubled over on the floor, in a cell across the hall. "Watch her rot, Guardian."

"No! Do anything you want to me, just bring her back." He frantically searched his brain for a way to appeal to Theodora, something to offer in exchange for Rhianna's life and freedom. "Take me instead. Let her go home."

"I already have you," Theodora snapped, her face glowing. "And you had your chance." She slammed and locked the metal cell door, a cage made up of heavy, thick bars. "Too bad. It would have been so much fun to have watched you in battle. It's all about the game," she mumbled as she headed for the door. "All about the game…" She turned with a swish of fabric and disappeared.

"Rhianna," Aidan bellowed as he darted to the cell door. He grabbed ahold of his own bars and looked over at her fallen body. A wild, ferocious growl ripped from his lungs. Then he took a few deep breaths.

Calm down. Think.

He glanced around to find there were no windows. He beat his fists on the walls. Were they solid, or could this all be an illusion Theodora had created? Pain shot into his hand, and his knuckles came away bloodied.

This was no illusion. His gaze settled on the metal grid of the doors. Could he squeeze through in his eagle form? He gritted his teeth in determination.

Changing to his eagle, he chose one of the lower sections to try slipping through. He got his head through but his shoulders hung up. The space was too small. He compressed his wings against his body. Damn, he still didn't fit. He wished he could grow smaller in the same way he grew larger, but his gifts didn't work like that. He pushed forward, wincing as shoulder feathers tore free. He took shallow breaths, looking across at Rhianna, who was still unconscious on the floor.

He needed to hurry.

Exhaling the air from his lungs, he pushed his body harder, squeezed smaller, so much so that his shoulder broke with a *snap* and his wing collapsed under the force.

He clenched his jaw, trying to distract himself from the agony of the break.

At last, able to squeeze his broken body through the square space, he came out the other side into the hall.

Breathing hard but not willing to stop, he repeated the process of going through Rhianna's cell door. It would be quicker this time, since his wing was already broken; it was only a matter of enduring the pain.

In her cell, he immediately took his human form again and began CPR. His broken arm was practically useless, but he stretched her out on her back with his good arm. He positioned his good hand on her chest and began compressions. Leaning over her, he placed his mouth on hers, breathing for her and forcing air into her lungs. He repeated the sequence several times until she responded with a sharp gasp. Her eyelids fluttered, and she filled her lungs several more times, then looked at him and smiled tremulously.

A wet, throaty laugh rumbled through him, he was so relieved.

At last, he collapsed against the wall, pulling her to him. He had never felt anything better.

18

The dungeon was silent except for the sound of their heavy breathing as they sat, leaning on each other. *Thank God he's okay.* She reached across and placed her hand on top of his. "I'm not sure what happened, but thank you."

Aidan twisted, groaning, and kissed her temple. "Theodora struck you with her dark magic and killed you. I revived you."

She chuckled. "Leave it to you to give me the condensed version."

He shrugged, his face scrunching in pain.

"What's wrong?" she asked. "Are you hurt?" She angled away from him to get a better look.

"Broke my shoulder," he said through clenched teeth. He came to his knees and stood, helping her to her feet with his good arm. "Now that you're okay, I'm going to go after her. We have to get that scepter and get out of here."

"I can help."

"I'll have to go through the door again. I'll come back

for you once I have the key." Wrapping his uninjured arm around her, he kissed her with longing. When they parted, his lips tugged into a lopsided smile. "Just in case Theodora does permanent damage this time."

She pulled him closer and kissed him again. "You figure a way out of this, and then we'll need to talk."

"Deal," he said, stepping back.

Rhianna sunk her teeth into her lip as he morphed into an eagle, made himself impossibly small, and squeezed through the bars of the door. On the other side, he changed back.

"Your arm," she said. "How will you fight her injured like that?"

"I heal rapidly. It will be fine." He gave her one last look of yearning, and then his hurried steps were echoing down the corridor. Eventually the footfalls disappeared altogether, leaving her in silence.

Rhianna stood in the middle of the empty cell. She hugged her arms around her middle and began to pace. At least it was better to listen to her footsteps than the silence. She paused at the door and glanced down the corridor. What had Aidan encountered when he'd left?

She jerked and pushed on the door, hoping it would miraculously open. It didn't. If only she could unlock it somehow. Her eyes swept the floor of the cell, looking for anything she could use to try to pick the lock. She pursed her lips, then gasped. She'd had a bobby pin earlier!

Maybe...

She patted her hair, and her fingers struck the thin slip of metal. *Yes!* She pulled the clip free of her hair.

Fiddling with the pin, she tried to recall the video about picking locks she'd watched years ago after locking herself out of her apartment.

First, bend the bobby pin back and forth until it breaks in half. Then, bend one of the halves at the tip.

Taking a deep breath, she reached her arms through

the metal grates. The cold bars nudged her chest. Since the lock was on the other side of the door, she'd be working blind, just by feel.

She put the bent end in place first and then added the other half in the lock above it. She jiggled the pin. After several attempts, she had to stop and rest. Her arms were cramping from having to hold them up at an awkward angle. But it didn't matter how long it took or how tired she got, she had to keep trying.

On the fourth attempt, the lock gave, and the door inched open. She could have squealed with joy. She'd done it!

But she had to be discreet. So she exited the dungeon cell as quietly as she could.

Once Aidan left Rhianna, he moved cautiously through the castle, taking his time to allow his shoulder at least some time to mend before confronting Theodora. He traveled along the main floor, peeking in doorways to various rooms—kitchen, dining room, living room, library. The castle was cavernous and empty.

He moved up the curved staircase to the second floor. There was a surprising lack of artwork for a place this size, leaving the walls bare. His footfalls were muffled by the thick rugs as he walked along the hallway, again tipping his head through every doorway. Each time, he held his breath, knowing Theodora could be within. At the end of a hall, he came to a room with tall double doors. *A distinguishing sign,* he thought.

He hesitated, rotating his shoulder. It was still painful, but it was usable. Controlled and careful, he turned the doorknob and looked in. The lighting was dim, even yellowed inside. Pushing the door wider, he inched through the threshold.

She was there in her bedroom, standing in her undergarments. Thick slashes covered her shoulders, ribs, and back, scars that spoke of being on the losing side of a sword fight.

He skimmed the room. No mirrors. Perhaps she didn't want reminders.

But the scepter lay on the bed not far from her.

Since she was still turned away from him, he slinked into the room. He was about as close to the scepter as she was now, and he swallowed hard.

As he stepped toward the bed, she turned with a hiss. "How dare you?" Her entire body was shaking with rage, and she lunged for her scepter.

Aidan crouched, then sprang forward, transforming into his tiger in midair as he leaped. His huge paws hit her square in the chest, knocking her back. He jumped again, this time to the bed, changing back to his human form with seamless ease.

He reached out and swept up the staff without breaking momentum and rolled off the bed, landing on his feet. Even with the scepter in his hand, unease ran rampant through him. Until it was destroyed, there was always the chance she could get ahold of it again. He would have smashed it on the ground if not for his uncertainty about whether he needed it to get out of this blasted universe or not. And he needed to accomplish that first.

As if fleeing a dangerous animal, he backed up quickly. The door was only a few feet away.

Just a little farther.

Theodora rose and spun around, grabbing something from the dresser. A red-stoned ring, he noted, as she slid it on her finger. She touched the stone, and it began to glow. She extended her hand, and the room began to move. Things shifted just as they had when he'd ended up in the dungeon.

He eyed the scepter in his hand. "But…but how?"

He heard footsteps coming up behind him and then Rhianna was bursting through the door.

"The ring!" she shouted. "We need to get the ring!"

He glanced back to Theodora. The ring was still glowing—the true source of her power.

Rhianna took two long strides, the second landed her on the bed and then she vaulted off the other side.

"No!" His heart rose in his chest, pushing into his throat. Theodora had already taken her life before. He couldn't stand to watch it happen again.

The room was moving as if it were a boat on a stormy sea. Rhianna cartwheeled over to Theodora with seeming ease. She had executed the move so fast, Aidan couldn't believe what he'd seen. She grabbed Theodora's arm and held it over her head.

Theodora twisted and struggled to touch the ring with her free hand to no avail. "Let go of me," she snarled.

In a blink of an eye, Rhianna reached up and removed the ring, gliding it from Theodora's finger and into her closed fist. The room instantly stilled.

"Run!" he yelled, even as pride filled his chest.

Rhianna darted over the bed again and out the door in front of him.

Theodora ranted at their backs, her voice shaking with fury. "The Demon Prince will hunt you down. The ring is mine; Riam is mine. You *cannot* leave." Theodora's cry of anguish bounced down the hall behind him, powerless.

Clutching the staff in one hand, Aidan ushered Rhianna forward with the other.

"We did it," she exclaimed.

He couldn't help but smile at her. "Now we just need to get out of this universe…"

They ran down the staircase. When her feet hit the landing, she halted, looking left and then right. "What happened to Katsu? Have you seen him?"

Aidan shook his head. "No. The last time I saw him was outside your chamber, before we were dumped in the dungeon."

"Do you remember where that was?" she asked.

He angled his head, thinking. "The other side of the library."

She nodded resolutely. "Let's go. I can't leave without him."

Aidan's jaw tensed, and he pulled back his shoulders. "Rhianna, we need to get out of here. We may have the scepter and the ring, but there is no telling if Theodora has other sources of destruction at her disposal."

"Please. If he's there, we'll take him with us. If not—" she swallowed hard, forcing the words out even though they were difficult to speak "—then we'll leave."

"Hurry," he bit out.

Aidan led the way to the appropriate room. The door was half-closed, and he pushed it opened. Rhianna sensed from the way his body stiffened that something was horribly wrong. She pushed her way in, stopping with her chest slammed up against Aidan's arm.

Her gaze darted straight to Katsu, who hung from a rope attached to a beam on the ceiling. She gasped, sharp pain radiating through her as her heart pounded hard against her breastbone.

"Is he…?" She couldn't bring herself to say it.

"Yes," he said, his voice soft and sad.

"Maybe we could use the scepter or ring to—"

"We can't bring him back." He placed his hand on her shoulder, looking into her eyes. "We don't know how to use these. For all we know they might not do anything but evil work. It's too risky."

She pressed her lips together, and her chin fell to touch

her chest. She knew he was right. But it hurt. God, it hurt. After all her great-grandfather had endured, after all this time, she had hoped to deliver him from this awful place. Hot tears slid down her cheeks.

Aidan walked over to Katsu, took him down, and rested him on the floor.

"I'm sorry," he said. "I wish there was more we could do"—he held his hand out for her to take—"but we must go."

Aidan led her from the castle, squeezing her hand in his. Now that the worst was over, she seemed exhausted. Her feet dragged with every step, her limps hanging loose. When they were outside, he paused. "You are too tired."

"No," she said faintly. "I can make it."

He presented her with the staff. "Here. Carry this. I'll change into my tiger and you can ride down the mountain."

Before she could protest, he transformed, stretching his muscles and testing his injured shoulder. It hurt a little but nothing he couldn't stand. Then he stood there, waiting for her to climb onto his back.

After a moment, she did.

Aidan broke into an easy run as Rhianna lowered her chest against him and held on. When he came to the drawbridge and the gorge below it, he jumped and changed into his eagle, taking care to keep her weight centered over his back. They soared for a mile or so, and then he returned to his tiger once more as they came into town.

People peered out the windows, and when they caught sight of a tiger and his woman, they ran into the streets. Aidan halted and changed to his human form. A buzz filled the air as the people around them whispered.

"Is that Theodora's staff?" one man finally asked.

"Yes. We have the staff and ring," Aidan told him. "And we're going to see if they will take us out of Riam and back to our world."

"Take us, too!" someone yelled.

"Yes, do not leave us here!" shouted another.

The crowd pushed against them. At the back of the group, Aidan spotted Steve, Sean, and Dillon.

Aidan held up both hands, palms out. "Wait. Wait. Anyone who wants to can come with us."

The people cheered and followed close behind as Aidan led them to the spot where they'd entered. Worry began to niggle in Aidan's belly. He wasn't sure how everyone was going to make the transition. Some of these people were very old. What effect would crossing over to the real world have on them, if any? Would it kill them instantly?

He quickly explained the situation to the group, and every person agreed to transfer out of this universe, no matter the consequences. No explanation was needed. Aidan understood the need to be released from this pain, this prison. In small groups, they silently joined hands.

"You took the ring from her, you should do the honors," Aidan said to Rhianna.

"I don't know if I can." She swept her tongue over her upper lip. "What if I mess up?"

"Just try," Dillon said. His words were followed by others, softly encouraging her.

Aidan leaned in and whispered in her ear so only she could hear. "No matter what happens, I love you. You can do this. I know it."

She pulled back and met his gaze with teary eyes. She simply kissed him and nodded.

Placing the ring on her hand, she touched it the way the sorceress had, running her index finger in a circle over the ring and then extending the scepter and repeating the same motion.

"Concentrate on our destination," she told them all.

The dirt and soil swirled up in the air and turned over. A bubble-like capsule appearing, catching all four hundred of them and transporting them back to their world. When the bubble finally burst, the men and women fell to the earth, covering his entire front yard. As they stood, it reminded him of the rock concerts he'd seen in movies.

A boisterous round of whoops and whistles sounded.

"Look," Rhianna said, her voice full of awe. "Color."

Aidan tipped his head back, looking up at the blue, blue sky and the shades of green of the foliage around them. He smiled and rained hot kisses over her face and mouth.

As they both came up for air, he realized he had a little problem. He had four hundred people on his deserted island.

He turned to face Dillon. "I leave it up to you to get these people off my island." He turned then and tromped into the forest, tugging Rhianna with him. They'd just made it beyond sight of the crowd when a dog's bark floated through the trees.

"Takeshi!" Rhianna cried. The dog came bounding at them, jumping up and pawing at their legs. He went from Rhianna to Aidan and then back to Rhianna.

"Easy," she said with a laugh. "You don't have to get so excited. We're home."

A warm feeling settled in his chest. Had she just called this home?

19

"Do you think you can stand the peace and quiet?" Aidan asked Rhianna as they stretched on the grassy bridge overlooking the waterfall. It was a warm day for late October, and the sun shone high overhead. The perfect day for a picnic.

"Oh yeah." She laughed. "I'm finished with excitement in my life."

He smiled. He and Rhianna were finally alone on the island once more. Seth had left the minute they'd returned, and while it had taken them four days and multiple trips to get everyone off his island, they were all gone.

Dillon had even agreed to cancel the TV show and had relinquished all footage to Aidan. Given what they had been through, Dillon didn't even bemoan the loss of the money he'd already spent, and he hadn't seemed in too big of a hurry to begin another "adventure."

"I'm taking a vacation," he'd told Aidan and Rhianna as he boarded the yacht they'd managed to retrieve. The coast guard found the vessel floating unmanned in the pacific.

Rhianna hadn't quite decided her next course of action. She only knew she needed time to think, time to explore her feelings for Aidan without the threat of death hanging over them, time to decide what, besides her grandfather, was truly important to her.

When they were in Riam, everything had been so intense, so black-and-white.

"What do you think happened to Theodora?" she asked, rolling to her side.

He shrugged. "Who knows. As far as I can guess, she will remain in that universe forever. *Alone.*" He had stored the ring and scepter deep within the Divine Tree where no one would get it.

She looked into his eyes and smiled. She had fallen in love with him. There was no denying it now.

Takeshi took a running leap over both Aidan and Rhianna. "Hey, you almost knocked me down," she squealed as the dog ran into the woods. "I don't need grass in my teeth."

Aidan stretched over her. "Let me see." He pretended to examine her mouth and then zoomed in for a kiss. She giggled.

"I like it when you laugh," he said. Then he leaned in and kissed her again.

His lips were firm, and he tasted like the oranges they'd eaten. Rhianna snuggled closer, gravitating toward his warmth and running her hands over his solid, muscular shoulders. She kissed him back, harder and more demanding. She wanted more of him, all of him.

He pulled back, and they both caught their breath. "I believe we have a promise to fulfill," he said.

"That's my understanding," she whispered, leaning into him. There were many things she wanted to forget about their experience in Riam, but the sultry kiss they'd shared in the Falcon station wasn't one of them. When they'd vowed to love another day.

He slid his hand under her top and smoothed his fingers across her ribs. She purred, and he groaned. That one delicious touch was all it took to start clothes flying in all directions.

He shoved the picnic items aside and gently guided Rhianna down onto the blanket in just her bra and panties. "You look so delectable. And I'm a very hungry man."

"Just a man?" she teased, looking at him from beneath her lashes.

"Okay…a shape-shifter," he corrected in a reluctant tone.

"Immortal," she said with pride.

His brows came together, and he pulled back. "Maybe we shouldn't…"

She grabbed his shoulders and pulled him to her. "I love everything you are."

His frown faded, and he stood up. Without fuss of fanfare, he stripped off his pants. She swallowed, barely stifling a gasp.

Wouldn't you know it? He's a commando man.

Her heartbeat raced at the sight of his magnificent body, sleek and muscular. He was a warrior. *Her* warrior.

With a tiger's grace, he knelt and ran his fingers along her jaw, down her neck, and over her breasts, pausing to admire her. She loved the intensity in his hazel eyes, the way they turned several shades darker as they flashed his longing for her. He slipped a finger along the smooth edge of her shirt and eased it down, exposing one of her breasts. She hissed in a breath, and he growled.

He glanced up, meeting her eyes. "You are incredibly beautiful."

So was he. She undid the front clasp of her bra, and his gaze followed her hands. As her breasts fell free, he wet his lips.

"I love you." She paused, hoping he felt the same and his earlier declaration hadn't just been the stress of the moment. "I want you so much."

He pulled back. Her words were so much more than he had ever hoped for. That someone would want him, maybe even want to end his loneliness... It was almost more than he could process. His heart squeezed with the desire that it would be so.

His hunger for her stirred, and his beasts seemed to be waiting at the corner of his heart to see if she would really give herself completely to him. A shape-shifter. An immortal. A misfit in her world.

The move had to be her choice. He would not force her to live in his isolated world. He cared about her too much for that.

As if sensing his hesitation, she wrapped her arms around his neck. "Don't pull away from me."

He had no more defenses against her. The dam in his heart burst, and he covered her mouth with a scorching, passionate kiss. Her breasts, soft and giving, pressed against his bare chest. He moved his hand to her ribs, then waist, and rolled so she was on top of him.

Barely breaking the kiss, she straddled him, taking control and delving her tongue deeper. Sitting up, she guided him, allowing him to kiss and suckle her gorgeous breasts. She moaned and rocked her hips. He slid his hand between them, finding that sweet spot beneath her panties, and rubbed his thumb there. She threw her head back with a moan.

Jesus, she was hot and ready for him. He couldn't wait a second longer. He smoothly rolled her onto her back again, slid her panties off, and positioned himself above her. She touched him, to help glide him into her. His body trembled; every sensation was nearly too much.

He moved inside her, and she wrapped her legs around his hips, pushing deeper, driving him crazy as he set a rhythm to take her higher. His jaw tensed with control. He wanted her pleasure to come first. He wanted to meld with her, to touch her soul as she had his.

Damp with perspiration, she groaned deep in her throat as he thrust into her. Her sweet body pulsed around his cock, sending him over the edge to climax with her.

As they clung to each other in exhaustion, Aidan allowed the thought to cross his mind of how good his life would be if she were in it. He rolled onto his side, holding her tight and taking her with him.

20

Takeshi came bounding back, interrupting the quiet aftermath of their love-making and her thoughts about how incredible it had been, how she wanted to be with Aidan for the rest of her life. The trouble was…he hadn't asked her to stay.

The pup growled, showing off the shoe in his mouth. She laughed. It was the one that she'd lost when she'd first arrived—or perhaps he'd stolen it.

"Hey, that's mine," she said as he ran by her. Aidan kissed her once more, before letting her go.

The dog darted around them as they threw on their clothes and then it took off again, still carrying her shoe.

Aidan called to the pup, but he didn't listen. "I should just let him run it off," he said.

Instead, they followed Takeshi. Aidan tracked him to Rhianna's first campsite on the island. She glanced around at where she'd made a fire and where she'd slept. The Mylar blanket was tucked neatly beneath the ledge, forgotten.

"Oh my goodness. It seems so long since I arrived," she said in a flash of memory.

Aidan came up behind her and circled his arm around her waist. She turned her head, and his lips brushed hers. "You were watching over me even then," she said.

"Not exactly." He smiled. "I wanted you to leave my island."

She licked her lips and raised an eyebrow. "And now?"

"Now I never want you to leave." He turned her to face him so they were nose to nose and she could see the sincerity in his eyes. "I've always thought I'd live my life alone. And I always have. But since meeting you... I don't want that anymore. I want to have someone to share things with. But I won't make you stay. You can come and go as you please."

Rhianna smiled as her heart skipped wildly against her ribs. "I think that's the most I've ever heard you say at once."

Aidan's mouth fell open. He shut it and scowled. "I pour my heart out, and that's all you have to say?"

She dipped her chin and looked at him out of the corner of her eyes. "That's not pouring your heart out."

He hesitated, seeming to think. He didn't seem amused that she'd boxed him in. "I love you, Rhianna. I want you to stay. I want you happy. I want you—"

She threw her arms around his neck and kissed him. "I love you, too, you crazy Guardian."

Aidan kissed her again as Takeshi decided he was finished playing hard to get and came over and sat at their feet, her shoe still in his mouth.

"Now if only my grandfather could spend his last days here, to see the beauty and the peace of this place, everything would be perfect," she said wistfully.

"That can be arranged," Aidan promised.

Epilogue

Moloch, the Demon Prince, stood on a hill within sight of
the Divine Tree. He watched the Guardian Aidan, the old
man, and the woman. It was thirty-two degrees out, and
they were doing some exercise in unison on the lawn.

Idiots.

He rarely if ever ventured to freezing climates in
December.

But never matter. That was not why he was here. Aidan
and the woman had taken the ring and scepter from
Theodora, and he intended to get it back. Eventually. Just
not in the freezing winter.

He pulled his mink coat tighter around him. At the
moment, he had a date with a foxy feline in Peru. But
before he headed there, he intended to leave Aidan a little
taste of what was to come. He set the three-foot-square
box on a nice, flat rock.

The box shifted sideways. The snake must be extremely
unhappy to be thrashing about violently enough to cause

such a movement. Then again, the snakes of the Dark Realm didn't appreciate being transferred earth side. It would strike whoever opened the box. Moloch didn't care whether it was the humans or Aidan who did the deed. Any and all would cause Aidan heartache.

Aidan should find it relatively quickly. His tiger should have the skills, even if the man didn't.

He narrowed his eyes on the woman.

Rhianna. Such a pretty little thing.

Too bad he couldn't stick around and watch. But he would know the outcome through *Migda*, the supernatural path of connections and networking within the Dark Realm. Yes, the snake would let him know when the deed was done.

THE END

Thank you for reading *Awakening Storm*. If you enjoyed this story and want to stay up-to-date on my next book and release dates then sign up for my newsletter. (I promise your email address will never be shared and you can unsubscribe at any time.)

https://larissaemerald.wordpress.com/contact/

Did you know that one of most awesome things you can do for an author is post a review? It doesn't need to be long, just a few lines will do, but a review goes a long way to help authors achieve visibility. So, if you enjoyed the book, share the news with a friend and take a few minutes to leave a review!

Read on for a sneak peek of

FOREVER AT DAWN

Available now.

Excerpt from

FOREVER AT DAWN
by Larissa Emerald

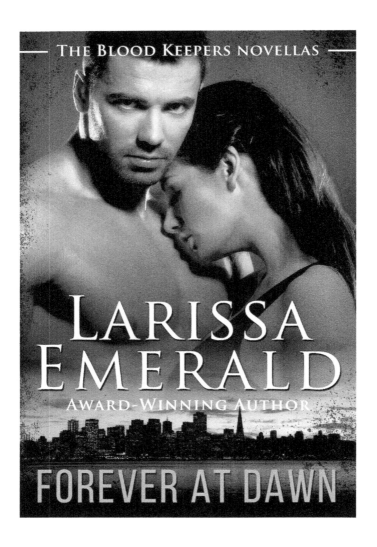

Chapter One

The wind coming off the Pacific created a sad, hollow whistle as it whipped upward along the stone walls of the mansion and hit the eves. Connor Langley peered out the window to sea.

"I'm traveling through the porthole this evening," he said.

He turned to look at Gavin. Connor's personal assistant drew himself taller and angled his gray head. "Isn't that dangerous with the impending storm?"

"Not really." Best not to get him worked up.

Gavin pursed his lips as if withholding a comment. The vampire no doubt knew he couldn't dissuade Connor.

"Don't fret. I won't be gone more than a day our time. I am simply going to bring back the mined cobine crystal our people need." He clenched his hands into fists and held back the growl at his lips. "To replenish the stores that were stolen."

"I take it the artificial manufacturing hasn't produced results."

Connor shook his head. "Unfortunately, no."

Over the years, vampires had led the way producing artificial diamonds, and rubies, and other precious gemstones—things humans seemed to be ecstatic over—

in an effort to reproduce a synthetic cobine. But the precious substance abundant on their home planet of Cest eluded their scientists. And it was a substance his race needed to survive, much as humans needed salt. An item extremely valuable to them, not just to wear and show off but to prevent them from feeding on humans.

He began to pace the room, fists tight by his sides. A cobine deficiency in vampires meant brain swelling, coma, and acute blood loss. Such a state would produce a feeding frenzy beyond reason to compensate for the deficit. It was up to each Czar to care for his region to ensure that didn't happen. The cobine he had procured eleven months ago should have sufficed for years, and yet the supply was critically low once again. He needed to move fast.

"Take me with you," Gavin suggested. "I'm good with horses."

Connor hid his surprise but could easily guess where the comment was coming from. What vampire wouldn't desire to go back in time to a simpler existence? "I will not remain there, Gavin, no matter how much I'd like to. Nor will you. I will not desert my people."

"It's become an obsession, this traveling back in time," Gavin warned.

Connor looked down at his clothes as his fangs descended. He inhaled a calming breath. "The world was so different then. The blood purer."

"Ah. I was wrong, you're not just obsessed... You're addicted, and—" his brows shot upward.

Waving a hand, Connor cut him off. "Like hell."

"Then send someone else."

Connor strode into the massive closet, making it clear the conversation was over. He dressed in jeans, a button-down shirt, and boots. It was time to find out who'd dared steal from him. And why.

In the past, he'd always known his enemy, and death occurred daily. But today, the battle was more mental and strategic. That's not to say there wasn't bloodshed. It just had to be with good reason.

When Connor walked back out of the closet, Gavin was staring at his watch, seemingly deep in thought. His old friend glanced up, and Connor tried to reassure him. "When I return, I'll increase our efforts to find another source so we aren't dependent on a past portal anymore. Perhaps it's time for a visit to London. And you can accompany me then." He slung on his period topcoat. "Except for the cobine, there is nothing in that time I can't leave."

Gavin gave a reluctant nod. "Something happens every time you go back. I can't explain it... I... I just feel the disengagement. It's like a fracture."

Yes, Connor knew what the man meant. But leaders had to stand strong and endure. He needed to help his people by doing the very best with the talents given to him.

Gavin crossed his arms over his thin chest. "You need to find the right woman to make you settle down," he blurted out.

"Where the hell did that come from?"

"Well, it's true. If you were in love, perhaps you'd stay at home."

His servant must truly be aging to bring up the subject of mating. "That's absurd. Besides, women are too much trouble. In all these centuries, I haven't found my destined mate."

"Obviously." Gavin cleared his throat and nodded with conviction. "Or else she'd be here to stop you now. Once you meet her, the mating thrall will take care of the rest."

Connor had heard enough. "I'll see you tomorrow." He spun on his heel and exited the room, taking the hall that led to the west end of the mansion.

In the den, he paused at the old mantle clock that rested on a pedestal table. He grabbed the small boy-with-horse figurine at its right, opened the clock case, and placed it inside, just out of range of the pendulum. Once the case was closed again, he pushed on a hidden panel door that led down into a tunnel. It opened with only the slightest creaking sound and he stepped inside.

The motion sensors noted his presence as he progressed, the lights coming on to guide him to the cavern he sought. The familiar wet, musty smell welcomed him.

At the base of a boulder, he knelt and removed the top of the largest stalagmite. The inside had been meticulously carved out to conceal the time rod. He removed the transporter piece, which resembled a long stained glass pen. He held it up to the light, pleased with the swirl of colors within, liquid energy beyond anything known to humans.

Warmth radiated through his body as he closed his fingers around it. Perhaps Gavin was right. He was addicted.

This was the connection to his past, the roots to his mother planet—the story of who his people were. Humans had named them "vampires" and the mysterious lore they'd created had not worked in his race's favor. Oddly, now they'd become popular. Indeed, his people were immortal, but not because of being undead. Yes, they fed on blood, and traced, and avoided daylight, but humans could never know the real truth.

There were truly evil beings walking the shadows of the Earth. In comparison, vampires were the good guys.

Connor fit the tip of the rod into the appropriate hole in the stratum of the rock, the vein that was formed in 1876. He forced the end in a little harder until a light ignited within the rod, causing the energy inside to swirl faster and heat up. He braced his palm against the rock wall above his head and closed his eyes, leaning in.

Impressions of this world, bits of light and a sense of the waves crashing on the shore, streamed by in a dizzying blur, with a rumble of friction so enormous it knocked him off his feet, his consciousness fading.

He awoke to the dripping of water landing on his ear. He shivered, shook his head, pushed to his elbows, and regained his bearing. He'd had the mansion built in the early eighteen hundreds and lived in it ever since. *Lifetime ownership.* He snickered at the thought and smiled as he stood. It was his favorite of several homes he owned around the globe.

He took the steps two at a time as he exited the cavern. When he reached the ground floor, he checked the clock. No figurine whatsoever. Good deal.

He really didn't want to engage the staff just yet, so he immediately traced to his office in the hotel he owned on Main Street. He deposited his coat on the coatrack. First order of business, he needed to track down the whereabouts of his mine foreman. It was a Friday, so he should be in town. Connor scribbled out a message, requesting the employee to meet with him, and went in search of an errand boy.

"It's stuck," a man yelled from outside, his voice wafting in through the window. Out of habit, Connor straightened his clothes. Not that anything was out of place. It was just what he did.

A few more people shouted, and Connor made his way out front to discover what the ruckus was about.

"Mornin', Mr. Langley," a housekeeper said as he passed. "I didn't know you was back."

Connor tipped the brim of his hat, shifting into the mannerisms of the day as easily as he traced.

Standing in the lobby, he looked outside. Even as people gathered on the steps in front of his hotel to take cover from the rain, he breathed in the freedom of the era.

No hidden cameras, or paparazzi, or media pressure. A huge temptation.

No, he reminded himself. *Get the cobine and go home.*

A steady rain beat down on a hearse stuck in the mud. Perhaps he should lend a hand. He wouldn't find this sort of action back in present time, that's for sure. So he set aside his hat and coat, tucking the message inside the folds to keep it dry and handed it to one of the hotel staff to hold for safe keeping. He rolled up his sleeves, loosened his collar down to the second button, and stepped out into the rain.

CHAPTER TWO

"Take heart, Steph. I can see the hotel from here."

Stephanie Davenport glanced sideways at her "cousin." Eric Bronson wasn't truly a relative but a close childhood friend who had agreed to accompany her on this cross-country adventure. At fifteen, she'd had an enormous crush on him, especially so after he'd been the first man to kiss her with tongue. The thought still made her stomach do flip-flops. But to her great disappointment, they'd only had the one encounter, and even though she'd no doubt looked at him with moon eyes every single time he'd returned home from college, he'd never kissed her again.

She sighed. The sunlight filtering through dreary, gray clouds was barely enough to highlight his golden flaxen hair and didn't do justice to his handsome features. At twenty-eight, and six years Stephanie's senior, Eric was a worldly man, and it showed in the way he spoke, walked, even smiled. She'd also caught the desirable way he'd glanced at some of the lovely women on their journey. She craved for a man to look upon her with such heat in his eyes. But she pushed those desires to the back of her mind. She was thankful he'd even agreed to accompany her on this journey to retrieve her inheritance.

She nodded to herself, focusing on the task at hand. It was time for her to strike out an independent path, and the money from selling her father's assets would turn into her best recourse. Beyond that, she wasn't sure where this escapade would lead.

A shiver of excitement mixed with unease skated down her spine.

Stephanie stomped the thick mud from her boots as she walked. She crinkled her nose, first at the muck, then at herself. She should be disgusted by her boldness. She was far from a gambler by nature. Yet here she was, after crossing the rough, untamed miles that stretched across America, tracking down a swindler named Connor Langley. The man her estranged father had empowered with her future.

A boisterous crowd lined Union Street, pulling her from her thoughts. Except for the steep, rocky hills, the scenery scarcely resembled the picture in the travel tome she clutched to her breast. She wasn't sure what she'd expected, but this place had a wild nature that New England didn't possess.

She hugged the book closer, comforted by the small roll of bills she'd tucked into her bodice as it scraped her sensitive skin. She sighed. At least she had return train fare.

The coach driver had dumped them in the drizzling rain, minus their luggage, on a covered walkway at least a block away from their hotel. "The driver said he'd deliver our belongings when he could get through," Eric shouted over the din.

She leaned closer to Eric to avoid yet another unladylike event. "There seems to be quite a commotion."

Eric took hold of her elbow. "Let's move on, shall we?" Angling an umbrella over them, they slipped between bystanders.

Odors—rich and heavy—of fish and oysters, wine, and baking bread, mingled with the salty wind from the Pacific, reminding her once more that they were a long way from Connecticut.

Stephanie mimicked Eric's motions, craning her head this way and that, glancing through the clusters of people lining the muddy street. What exactly had prevented their carriage from reaching the hotel? Why the crowd?

Eric tugged her along for a few steps, and she resisted the urge to pull free. It wasn't until they reached the elevated safety of the hotel's covered porch—her dear departed father's hotel, she noted with great relief because they'd finally arrived—that she discovered the attraction.

There, right in front of the hotel, smack dab in the center of the roadway and skewed sideways, was a huge black hearse with a set of four equally coal-black horses, a man built as strong as a buffalo by its side.

For an instant, she expected a villain to emerge from the darkened doorway and brand the man hammering the carriage wheel with his fist a fool. But a funeral hearse didn't harbor villains, she immediately corrected, and when the man stretched to his full height, her heart jolted. No, this man wasn't a fool, she thought as she tried to work her suddenly dry throat. His stance revealed pride and distinction.

"Oh my," she finally said, astonished. "That man is half-naked!"

She shivered. He was practically shirtless, and drops of rain trickled over his wide, pale shoulders where his shirt had been torn half off of him. A smear of mud drew her attention to the well-defined muscles of his broad chest. Water mixed with the wet earth, and she watched, eyes wide, as the brown silt traveled that long, hard path to the waistband of his trousers. Farther south, rain-soaked black fabric clung to his powerful thighs, emphasizing a physique obviously familiar with hard work.

Certainly, the pictures of Hercules in her books on Greek mythology were no comparison to the living, breathing specimen, heroically laboring to raise the vehicle from the mud. Her face flushed hot. Was it sinful to watch him?

Her fellow educators at Hartford Girls' School would undoubtedly think so.

The man turned his head, and drops of water flung from the ends of his dark hair. Stephanie frowned. It didn't bother him in the least that he was the crowd's entertainment. In fact, it was as if he was reveling it in.

His gaze met hers and held. Her first instinct was to turn away, but she couldn't. Instead, she brazenly returned his gaze. Her heart thrummed in her chest. Why was he staring?

Then his brow creased and eyes narrowed, as if he recognized her and was trying to place her. But that was impossible, for this was her first—and last—visit to San Francisco. Besides, one didn't forget such breathtaking good looks.

Stephanie tore her gaze from Hercules, scanning the spectators. "Look at all the people, Eric," she said softly. "They remind me of an audience watching a carnival."

"Indeed. I imagine this to be the best entertainment in their monotonous lives."

She plucked at the high collar of her dress, assaulted by the persistent humidity and press of the crowd. "We should be going."

"In a minute. I want to see him in action."

Shamefully, so did she. Her pulse skipped and she nearly forgot to breathe when the handsome rescuer forced heavy boards into the muck beneath the front wheels of the hearse. He ordered the nearby men to take action. The coachman, still wearing his dripping-wet top hat, snapped a whip and urged the horses forward. Another man stepped out to assist in guiding the team.

The wood being used for leverage began to sink. The hearse tilted toward Hercules. Stephanie gasped right along with the crowd. He pressed both hands to the shiny, lacquered side of the vehicle and pushed until his arm and back muscles bulged from the effort. At her side, Eric took two steps forward, perhaps thinking to help, but several other men rushed in with the same intent. At last, the team lurched forward and sprang into motion with enough force to pull the coach free.

Relieved, Stephanie exhaled sharply. People clapped and cheered. A few rowdy men blasted ear-piercing whistles.

"For a minute there, I thought the poor man would be joining the one in the box," Eric joked. "Good thing he's a big fellow."

"Yes. He is, isn't he?" she agreed, studying the nearly unclad man. He had the elemental rawness of a man in close touch with nature, an intrinsic wildness that made her nervous, even frightened. She imagined him working the docks, cutting timber, or hefting masonry blocks. Whatever his occupation, his strength had served him well today.

A man pumped the rescuer's hand. "Good work, Mr. Langley."

Langley? She gasped and shook her head. *He can't be...*

Yet, another man called out his name. Good Heavens, Hercules wasn't a dockworker. The gorgeous man with muscles like she'd never seen before was her father's no-good, cheating partner.

Mud splashed about him with each step he took as Mr. Langley moved in her direction. Panic gripped her. She had no wish to greet the man disheveled as he was—no desire to be closer to his coarse manliness. Or maybe her desire was the problem.

The impulse to flee tore at her but a lifetime of fighting her own battles had taught her the necessity for supreme calm. "Eric, let's go inside and secure our room," she urged.

Eric held out his elbow to escort her when a tall fellow, with a small, scruffy dog tucked beneath one arm, burst between them, pushing them both off-balance. Stephanie tried to catch herself as momentum propelled her down the steps. The muck loomed in front of her. *No!* The cry caught in her throat just before she closed her eyes.

Her book flew from her hands and a jarring wrench vibrated through her when she hit something solid, immovable. But instead of landing in slimy mud, her hands descended on firm, slick skin, and her cheek rested against warm, wet smoothness. The scent of musky masculinity filled her nostrils. Unsure of her own senses, she moved her fingers up and down slowly, testing the texture. Hard muscles flexed beneath her palm, and her fingers ran over the edges of a torn, soaked shirt. She groaned in recognition. Opening her eyes, she beheld mud-splattered flesh.

Mr. Connor Langley.

Shock held her still. For an instant, a shameless part of her acknowledged that he felt wonderful, protective, and this seemed a good place to rest until her world settled. Then she returned to reality, recalling who it was she rested upon. She struggled to push away from him.

"Are you injured?"

His quiet baritone voice slipped through her defenses, touching a tender place in her heart. One strong arm encircled her waist, so close that she doubted even the rainwater could trickle between them. Her gaze traveled unbidden over muscular planes up to a square jaw and angular cheekbones until she met his cobalt-blue eyes.

He studied her with concerned intensity, two deep lines furrowing between his eyes. Though she knew he was only worried about her safety, Stephanie couldn't get past the raw sensuality of being so near him, or the strange melting sensation that settled low in her abdomen.

Finally, she recalled his question. "No... No, I'm fine," she whispered. Then, finding her customary sturdier voice, she added, "if you would please let go of me."

He released her, and she recoiled from him like a person jumping away from a snake. She staggered backward until her heel hit the edge of the steps. Giving her hands a shake, she forced them into the folds of her dress and cleared her throat.

But all the while she simply wanted to slip right back into those strong arms.

AVAILABLE NOW

ACKNOWLEDGMENTS

Many thanks to my fabulous team of professionals:

Cover design: The Killion Group, Inc.
Interior formatting: Author E.M.S.
Editor: Daniel Poiesz, Double Vision Editorial

About the Author

Larissa Emerald has always had a powerful creative streak whether it's altering sewing patterns, or the need to make some minor change in recipes, or frequently rearranging her home furnishings, she relishes those little walks on the wild side to offset her otherwise quite ordinary life. Her eclectic taste in books cover numerous genres, and she writes sexy contemporary romance, paranormal romance, and futuristic romantic thrillers. But no matter the genre or time period, she likes strong women in dire situations who find the one man who will adore her beyond reason and give up everything for true love.

Larissa is happy to connect with her readers. Stop by and say hello at her website, Facebook, Twitter, or send her an email: larissaemerald@gmail.com.